Les Misérables

悲慘世界

Original Author   Victor Hugo
Adaptor   Michael Robert Bradie
Illustrator   An Ji-yeon

WORDS
800

MP3

Let's Enjoy Masterpieces!

All the beautiful fairy tales and masterpieces that you have encountered during your childhood remain as warm memories in your adulthood. This time, let's indulge in the world of masterpieces through English. You can enjoy the depth and beauty of original works, which you can't enjoy through Chinese translations.

The stories are easy for you to understand because of your familiarity with them. When you enjoy reading, your ability to understand English will also rapidly improve.

This series of *Let's Enjoy Masterpieces* is a special reading comprehension booster program, devised to improve reading comprehension for beginners whose command of English is not satisfactory, or who are elementary, middle, and high school students. With this program, you can enjoy reading masterpieces in English with fun and efficiency.

This carefully planned program is composed of 5 levels, from the beginner level of 350 words to the intermediate and advanced levels of 1,000 words. With this program's level-by-level system, you are able to read famous texts in English and to savor the true pleasure of the world's language.

The program is well conceived, composed of reader-friendly explanations of English expressions and grammar, quizzes to help the student learn vocabulary and understand the meaning of the texts, and fabulous illustrations that adorn every page. In addition, with our "Guide to Listening," not only is reading comprehension enhanced but also listening comprehension skills are highlighted.

In the audio recording of the book, texts are vividly read by professional American actors. The texts are rewritten, according to the levels of the readers by an expert editorial staff of native speakers, on the basis of standard American English with the ministry of education recommended vocabulary. Therefore, it will be of great help even for all the students that want to learn English.

Please indulge yourself in the fun of reading and listening to English through **Let's Enjoy Masterpieces**.

維克多・雨果

Victor Hugo
(1802~1885)

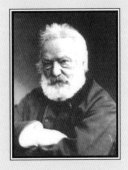

Victor Hugo was a famous French poet, novelist, and playwright. He was the third son in his family. His father was a high-ranking officer in Napoleon's army, and his mother was an extreme Catholic Royalist. Hugo was interested in literature, but his father wanted him to be a soldier.

Hugo published his first collection of poems, *Odes et Poésies Diverses*, in 1822. After that, he published several collections of poems, novels, and plays over a twenty-year period. After his daughter died in 1843, he focused on politics for the next ten years.

When Louis Napoleon seized power in 1851 and established an anti-parliamentary constitution, Hugo called him a traitor to France. Hugo left France and lived in exile for nineteen years, during which time he became absorbed in writing. His best works came from this period. The novel ***Les Misérables*** (1862), along with *Notre-Dame de Paris* (1831), is considered his best work.

Hugo died in Paris on May 22, 1885, at the age of 83. He was given a state funeral. Two million people in Paris mourned his death, and he was buried in the Pantheon.

Les Misérables, translated variously from the French title as *The Miserable Ones*, *The Poor Ones*, or *The Wretched Poor*, is considered one of the greatest novels of the 19th century. It consists of 5 volumes and 10 books.

This novel included Hugo's thoughts on social and religious life. Hugo wrote passionately about establishing an ideal society and worked hard for the wretched.

The main plot is about Jean Valjean, an ex-convict. Jean Valjean, a poor man, was once imprisoned for stealing a loaf of bread for his starving family. After being released from prison, he steals the Bishop Myriel's silverware and wants to get revenge on society. He is caught, but the bishop forgives him.

Finally, Valjean repents and begins a new life. Valjean becomes a wealthy factory owner and is appointed mayor of his adopted town.

But one day an innocent man is arrested and accused of being Jean Valjean. The man is going to be tried the next day. To save the innocent man, the real ex-convict decides to go to the trial and reveal his true identity. Valjean is promptly arrested. Imprisoned, Valjean soon escapes.

Later, he meets Fantine, who used to be a worker at his factory, and her daughter Cosette. Valjean saves Cosette from a life of prostitution, and they live happily together. Nevertheless, Inspector Javert keeps chasing Valjean . . .

HOW TO USE THIS BOOK
本書使用說明

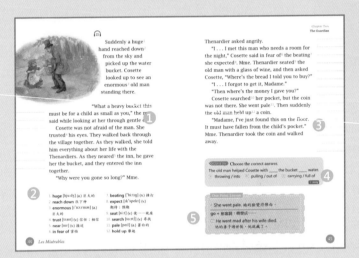

① Original English texts

It is easy to understand the meaning of the text, because the text is divided phrase by phrase and sentence by sentence.

② Explanation of the vocabulary

The words and expressions that include vocabulary above the elementary level are clearly defined.

③ Response notes

Spaces are included in the book so you can take notes about what you don't understand or what you want to remember.

④ One point lesson

In-depth analyses of major grammar points and expressions help you to understand sentences with difficult grammar.

∩ Audio Recording

In the audio recording, native speakers narrate the texts in standard American English. By combining the written words and the audio recording, you can listen to English with great ease.

Audio books have been popular in Britain and America for many decades. They allow the listener to experience the proper word pronunciation and sentence intonation that add important meaning and drama to spoken English. Students will benefit from listening to the recording twenty or more times.

After you are familiar with the text and recording, listen once more with your eyes closed to check your listening comprehension. Finally, after you can listen with your eyes closed and understand every word and every sentence, you are then ready to mimic the native speaker.

Then you should make a recording by reading the text yourself. Then play both recordings to compare your oral skills with those of a native speaker.

HOW TO IMPROVE READING ABILITY

如何增進英文閱讀能力

① Catch key words

Read the key words in the sentences and practice catching the gist of the meaning of the sentence. You might question how working with a few important words could enhance your reading ability. However, it's quite effective. If you continue to use this method, you will find out that the key words and your knowledge of people and situations enables you to understand the sentence.

② Divide long sentences

Read in chunks of meaning, dividing sentences into meaningful chunks of information. In the book, chunks are arranged in sentences according to meaning. If you consider the sentences backwards or grammatically, your reading speed will be slow and you will find it difficult to listen to English.

You are ready to move to a more sophisticated level of comprehension when you find that narrowly focusing on chunks is irritating. Instead of considering the chunks, you will make it a habit to read the sentence from the beginning to the end to figure out the meaning of the whole.

③ Make inferences and assumptions

Making inferences and assumptions is part of your ability. If you don't know, try to guess the meaning of the words. Although you don't know all the words in context, don't go straight to the dictionary. Developing an ability to make inferences in the context is important.

The first way to figure out the meaning of a word is from its context. If you cannot make head or tail out of the meaning of a word, look at what comes before or after it. Ask yourself what can happen in such a situation. Make your best guess as to the word's meaning. Then check the explanations of the word in the book or look up the word in a dictionary.

④ Read a lot and reread the same book many times

There is no shortcut to mastering English. Only if you do a lot of reading will you make your way to the summit. Read fun and easy books with an average of less than one new word per page. Try to immerse yourself in English as often as you can.

Spend time "swimming" in English. Language learning research has shown that immersing yourself in English will help you improve your English, even though you may not be aware of what you're learning.

CONTENTS

Introduction 4

How to Use This Book 6

How to Improve Reading Ability 8

Before You Read 12

Chapter One

Two Desperate Souls 14

Comprehension Quiz 30

Chapter Two

The Guardian 32

Comprehension Quiz 50

Understanding the Story 52
The Models of the Characters

Chapter Three

The Parisians 54

Comprehension Quiz 76

Chapter Four

The Lovers & Revolution 78

Comprehension Quiz 100

Understanding the Story 102
The Background for the Story

Chapter Five

Redemption 104

Comprehension Quiz 122

Appendixes

1 Basic Grammar 124
2 Guide to Listening Comprehension . 128
3 Listening Guide 132
4 Listening Comprehension 136

Translation 138

Answers 174

Before You Read

Jean Valjean

I spent[1] 19 years in prison[2], but now that I've gotten out[3], I want to change my life and become a good man. I try to help the poor[4] and take care of[5] my dear Cosette.

Cosette

I grew up[6] neglected[7] in the Thenardiers' inn[8], but Jean Valjean rescued[9] me. We have a happy life together, but we're always moving[10], like we're running from something.

---

1. **spend** [spend] (v.) 花費（時間）
   (spend-spent-spent)
2. **prison** ['prɪzən] (n.) 監獄
3. **get out** 出來
4. **the poor** 窮人
5. **take care of** 照顧
6. **grow up** 長大
7. **neglect** [nɪ'glekt] (v.) 忽視
8. **inn** [ɪn] (n.) 客棧
9. **rescue** ['reskjuː] (v.) 拯救
10. **move** [muːv] (v.) 搬家

Inspector Javert

I'm a policeman, and I've been chasing[11] Jean Valjean for years. Somehow[12], he always seems to[13] escape from[14] me, but I won't give up[15]. I'll find him if it's the last thing I do.

Marius

Even though[16] my grandfather and I don't get along[17] anymore, that's all right because I'm in love with[18] Cosette. I want to marry[19] her, but it's hard to find her since she and her father are always moving.

Thenardier

Ever since[20] Jean Valjean took Cosette from my inn, my family has been poor. I have to do many things, including[21] stealing[22], to get money for my family.

---

11. **chase** [tʃeɪs] (v.) 追捕
12. **somehow** [ˈsʌmhaʊ] (adv.) 不知怎地
13. **seem to** 似乎
14. **escape from** 自……逃離
15. **give up** 放棄
16. **even though** 即使

17. **get along** 和睦相處
18. **be in love with** 與……相愛
19. **marry** [ˈmæri] (v.) 結婚
20. **ever since** 自從
21. **include** [ɪnˈkluːd] (v.) 包括
22. **steal** [stiːl] (v.) 偷竊
    (steal-stole-stolen)

Chapter One

🎧 1

Two Desperate¹ Souls²

One cold evening in October of 1815, a man with a long beard³ and dirty clothes walked into the French town of Digne. The man was in his forties and very strong. He carried a bag and a walking staff⁴.

The man entered an inn and said to the innkeeper⁵, "I've been traveling for a long time, and I'm very tired. I need a meal and a place to sleep. I have money to pay you."

The innkeeper looked closely at the strange man. "I know who you are. You are Jean Valjean. You've just been released⁶ from prison⁷. I don't serve⁸ people like you! Get out of⁹ here immediately!"

---

1. **desperate** [ˈdespərɪt] (a.) 不顧一切的；絕望的
2. **soul** [soʊl] (n.) 靈魂
3. **beard** [bɪrd] (n.) 山羊鬍
4. **walking staff** 拐杖
5. **innkeeper** [ˈɪnˌkiːpər] (n.) 客棧老闆
6. **release** [rɪˈliːs] (v.) 釋放
7. **prison** [ˈprɪzən] (n.) 監獄
8. **serve** [sɜːrv] (v.) 接待
9. **get out of** 離開
10. **peacefully** [ˈpiːsfəli] (adv.) 平靜地
11. **lie down** 躺下
12. **wooden** [ˈwʊdn] (a.) 木製的
13. **difference** [ˈdɪfərəns] (n.) 差別

Jean Valjean left peacefully[10]. Outside it was dark, cold, and windy. He was desperate for a place to rest. He lay down[11] on a stone bench in front of a church and tried to sleep. But a woman came out and asked, "How can you sleep outside on that stone bench?"

"I've been sleeping on a wooden[12] one in prison for nineteen years. What's the difference[13]?"

One Point Lesson

I've been sleeping on a wooden one in prison for nineteen years.
我已經在牢裡的木板椅上睡了十九年了。

---

have been V-ing: 表示已經進行某個動作,或從事某個工作一段時間了

e.g. He **has been waiting** for you for two hours.
他已經等你兩個小時了。

The woman pointed to[1] a small house next to the church. "You could stay there," she said.

The Bishop[2] of Digne was a gentle[3], old man who lived with his sister and a servant[4]. He helped anyone who was in need, and he never locked his doors.

That evening, he was sitting by the fire when his sister said, "Brother, people are saying there's a terrible man in town. The police have told everyone to lock their doors and windows."

But the bishop only smiled. Suddenly there was a loud knock[5] at the door.

"Come in," said the bishop.

The bishop's sister and servant trembled[6] when Jean Valjean walked into their house, but the bishop was calm[7].

"I am Jean Valjean," said the stranger. "I've just been released from prison after nineteen years. I've been walking for four days, and I desperately need a place to rest. Can you help me?"

---

1. **point to** 指著
2. **bishop** [ˈbɪʃəp] (n.) 主教
3. **gentle** [ˈdʒentl] (a.) 和善的
4. **servant** [ˈsɜːrvənt] (n.) 僕人
5. **knock** [nɑːk] (n.) 敲門聲
6. **tremble** [ˈtrembəl] (v.) 發抖
7. **calm** [kɑːlm] (a.) 鎮定的
8. **warm oneself** 暖和自己身子
9. **monsieur** [məˈsjɜːr] (n.) 先生（法語）

The bishop told his servant to set another place at the table for Valjean. "Sit down, and warm yourself[8], Monsieur[9] Valjean," said the bishop. "Dinner will be ready soon."

✓ Check Up Fill in the blank with proper word.
Valjean found no place to _____ because he had just been released from prison.

Ans: rest

🎧 3

After the big meal, Valjean began to relax[1] and look around the small house. The bishop's house was not luxurious[2], but he could see the valuable[3] set of silver knives, forks, and candlesticks[4] at the table. Then he noticed the bishop's servant putting the silverware[5] away[6] in a cabinet[7].

The bishop handed[8] one of the candlesticks to Valjean. "Here, this will light[9] your way. Follow me to the spare[10] bedroom," said the bishop.

---

1. **relax** [rɪˈlæks] (v.) 放鬆
2. **luxurious** [lʌɡˈʒʊəriəs] (a.) 奢華的
3. **valuable** [ˈvæljʊəbəl] (a.) 值錢的
4. **candlestick** [ˈkændlˌstɪk] (n.) 燭台
5. **silverware** [ˈsɪlvərwer] (n.) 銀器

6. **put away** 收好;儲存
7. **cabinet** [ˈkæbɪnət] (n.) 櫥櫃
8. **hand** [hænd] (v.) 傳;遞
9. **light** [laɪt] (v.) 照亮
   (light-lit/lighted-lit/lighted)

Once they were in the room, the bishop said, "Good night. And don't forget to have a bowl of[11] our fresh cow's milk before you leave tomorrow."

Valjean was so tired that he fell asleep with his clothes on. But even though he was exhausted[12], he woke up only a few hours later. Unable to sleep, he brooded[13] about his past. Life had been terribly unfair[14] to him, and he was still furious[15] about it.

In 1795, Valjean had lost his job as a lumberjack[16]. But at that time he had been supporting[17] his widowed[18] sister and her seven children. He was caught stealing[19] loaves of[20] bread to feed[21] them and had lost the best years of his life for that.

10. **spare** [sper] (a.)
    剩餘的；空間的
11. **a bowl of** 一碗
12. **exhausted** [ɪgˈzɑːstɪd] (a.)
    筋疲力盡的
13. **brood** [bruːd] (v.) 沉思
14. **unfair** [ˌʌnˈfer] (a.) 不公平的
15. **furious** [ˈfjʊriəs] (a.) 憤怒的

16. **lumberjack** [ˈlʌmbərdʒæk] (n.)
    筏木工人
17. **support** [səˈpɔːrt] (v.) 資助
18. **widowed** [ˈwɪdoʊd] (a.) 守寡的
19. **steal** [stiːl] (v.) 偷竊
20. **a loaf of** 一條
21. **feed** [fiːd] (v.) 餵養
    (feed-fed-fed)

🎧 4

Valjean wanted revenge[1] on the whole world! Then he thought of the bishop's valuable silverware and thought of a plan.

Valjean got out of bed and moved quietly around the house with his shoes off. In his hand, he held[2] a short iron bar[3] that was sharp on one end. He went into the bishop's room and held the bar over the sleeping man's head. But the bishop's sleeping face looked so peaceful and kind that Valjean could not kill him. So he stuffed[4] the valuable silver knives and forks into his bag and escaped[5] by climbing through the garden in back of the house.

The next morning, the bishop was sadly examining[6] some flowers in the garden that had been damaged[7] during Valjean's escape.

"Bishop," cried his servant, "do you know that your precious silverware has been stolen? That man who stayed here last night must have taken it!"

1. **revenge** [rɪˈvendʒ] (n.) 復仇
2. **hold** [hoʊld] (v.) 握著 (hold-held-held)
3. **iron bar** 鐵條
4. **stuff** [stʌf] (v.) 塞（入）
5. **escape** [ɪˈskeɪp] (v.) 逃走
6. **examine** [ɪɡˈzæmɪn] (v.) 檢查
7. **damage** [ˈdæmɪdʒ] (v.) 損壞；破壞
8. **sergeant** [ˈsɑːrdʒənt] (n.) 警察小隊長
9. **criminal** [ˈkrɪmɪnəl] (n.) 罪犯

"Yes, I know," said the bishop. "But I think it was wrong of me to keep that expensive silverware for so long."

Later that morning, four policemen and Valjean came back to the bishop's house. "Bishop," said the police sergeant[8], "we caught this criminal[9] with some valuable silverware. Is it yours?"

The bishop smiled at Valjean, "Dear friend, you forgot to take these silver candlesticks. They will bring you at least 200 francs."

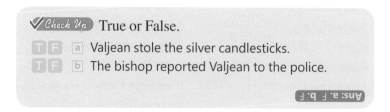

✔ *Check Up* True or False.

T F [a] Valjean stole the silver candlesticks.
T F [b] The bishop reported Valjean to the police.

Ans: a. F b. F

Valjean and the policemen's eyes widened[1] in disbelief[2]. "Sir, are you saying that you gave this silverware to this man?" asked the sergeant.

"Yes, absolutely[3]. You must let him go."

Then the policemen left. The bishop walked up close to Valjean and said, "Now you must use this money to make yourself an honest man. I've bought your soul from the devil[4] and given it to God."

Jean Valjean wandered[5] into the countryside feeling confused[6]. When the world had been unfair to him and he had been very angry, things had made sense to him. But now that[7] he had been shown such great kindness, he didn't know what to do.

Then as he crossed a large field, Valjean encountered[8] a ten-year-old boy. The boy was walking, whistling[9], and happily tossing[10] a silver coin into the air and catching it. Valjean held out his hand and caught the boy's coin.

---

1. **widen** [ˈwaɪdn] (v.) 變大
2. **in disbelief** 懷疑地
3. **absolutely** [ˌæbsəˈluːtli] (adv.) 絕對地
4. **devil** [ˈdevəl] (n.) 惡魔
5. **wander** [ˈwɑːndər] (v.) 徘徊
6. **confused** [kənˈfjuːzd] (a.) 困惑的
7. **now that** 既然……
8. **encounter** [ɪnˈkaʊntər] (v.) 遇到
9. **whistle** [ˈwɪsəl] (v.) 吹口哨
10. **toss** [tɒːs] (v.) 丟擲

"Please sir, give me my coin back. I'm just a chimney sweep[11], and it's all the money I have."

"Go away," said Valjean.

"But Monsieur . . . please!" cried the boy.

Valjean raised his stick to strike[12] the boy. The boy became very frightened[13] and ran away. Once the boy was out of sight[14], Valjean looked at the coin in his hand. He could not believe what he had done. He called for[15] the boy to come back, but the boy was gone. He sat down exhausted on a rock, and for the first time in nineteen years, he wept[16].

11. **chimney sweep**
    掃煙囪的工人
12. **strike** [straɪk] (v.) 打；擊
    (strike-struck-struck)
13. **frightened** [ˈfraɪtnd]
    (a.) 害怕的

14. **out of sight** 離開視線
15. **call for** 請求
16. **weep** [wiːp] (v.) 流淚
    (weep-wept-wept)

In the year 1818, in a small village named Montfermeil near Paris, two small girls were playing on a swing[1]. It was a lovely spring evening. Their mother was a plain-looking[2] woman with red hair. She sat nearby[3] watching them from in front of the small inn where they lived.

Suddenly a young woman approached[4] her and said, "Madam, your girls are very pretty."

The young woman was holding a sleeping child in her arms. But she looked poor and unhappy.

"Thank you," said the girls' mother. "Sit down, and take a rest[5]. You look tired."

The young woman sat down and introduced herself. Her name was Fantine.

"My name is Mme.[6] Thenardier," said the woman with two daughters. "My husband and I manage[7] this inn."

Fantine told the woman that she used to work in Paris, but her husband died, and she lost her job. But she was lying. In truth[8], she had gotten pregnant[9] by a young man who ran away[10]. It was very hard for unmarried[11] women with children at this time.

Then Fantine's little girl woke up. Her eyes were big and blue like her mother's. The little girl giggled[12] and jumped off her mother's lap. She ran to play with the two girls on the swing.

1. **swing** [swɪŋ] (n.) 鞦韆
2. **plain-looking** 長相平庸的
3. **nearby** [ˈnɪrbaɪ] (adv.) 附近地
4. **approach** [əˈproutʃ] (v.) 接近
5. **take a rest** 休息一下
6. **Mme. (Madame)** 太太；夫人（法語）
7. **manage** [ˈmænɪdʒ] (v.) 經營；管理
8. **in truth** 事實上
9. **pregnant** [ˈpregnənt] (a.) 懷孕的
10. **run away** 跑掉
11. **unmarried** [ʌnˈmærid] (a.) 未婚的
12. **giggle** [ˈgɪgəl] (v.) 咯咯地笑

"What's your daughter's name?" asked Mme. Thenardier.

"Her name is Cosette. She's nearly[1] three."

The two women watched their children playing together. Mme. Thenardier laughed, "Look at how easily they play. They could be sisters."

These words made Fantine do something very strange. Suddenly she grasped[2] the other woman's hand and asked, "Could you possibly take care of[3] her for me? I must find work, and it's almost impossible for a woman with a child and no husband. I'll get her as soon as I have a job. I have enough money to pay you six francs per month!"

Mme. Thenardier did not answer. She did not know what to say. But her husband was standing behind them. "We'll take care of her for seven francs a month if you pay six months in advance[4]."

Fantine took the money from her purse.

The next morning, Fantine said goodbye to her daughter, kissing her and crying as if her heart were breaking.

---

1. **nearly** ['nɪrli] (adv.) 幾乎地
2. **grasp** [græsp] (v.) 抓牢
3. **take care of** 照顧
4. **in advance** 預先
5. **M. (monsieur)** 先生（法語）
6. **debt** [dɛt] (n.) 負債
7. **avoid** [ə'vɔɪd] (v.) 避免
8. **trick** [trɪk] (v.) 詐騙
9. **intend to** 打算；有意要……
10. **reply** [rɪ'plaɪ] (v.) 回覆

"We need this money," said M.[5] Thenardier
to his wife. "Now I can pay my debts[6] and
avoid[7] going to prison. You did a good job
tricking[8] that lady."

"Although I hadn't intended to[9]," replied[10]
his wife.

One Point Lesson

I'll get her as soon as I have a job.
我一找到工作就會來接她。

as soon as + 主詞 + 動詞：一……就……

e.g. She ran away as soon as she saw me.
她一看到我就跑掉了。

A month later, M. Thenardier needed more money, so he sold Cosette's clothes for sixty francs. They dressed the little girl in rags[1] and made her eat scraps[2] of food under the table with the dog and the cat.

In the meantime[3], Fantine began working at a factory[4] in a city far away. She sent letters and money for her daughter every month. The Thenardiers began to ask for[5] more money, and Fantine gladly paid it. They told Fantine they treated[6] her daughter well. But in truth, while they treated their own daughters, Eponine and Azelma, very well, they treated little Cosette like a slave[7].

---

1. **rags** [rægs] (n.) 〔複〕破爛衣褲
2. **scraps** [skræps] (n.) 殘渣
3. **in the meantime** 此際;同時
4. **factory** [ˈfæktəri] (n.) 工廠
5. **ask for** 要求
6. **treat** [tri:t] (v.) 對待
7. **slave** [sleɪv] (n.) 奴隸
8. **keep A a secret** 將 A 事保密

Fantine was careful to keep her daughter a secret[8] at the factory where she worked. But the women there finally discovered[9] that she was an unwed[10] mother and told everyone. Fantine was fired[11] from her job and couldn't find another one anywhere.

That winter, Fantine went without a fire in her little room just to save[12] a little more money for Cosette. She earned a little money sewing[13] shirts, but it wasn't enough. She went to a wig-maker[14] and sold her hair for ten francs.

Then she got a letter from the Thenardiers saying that Cosette was very ill and needed forty francs for medicine[15]. This made Fantine very desperate. She sold her two front teeth.

After her hair and teeth were gone, Fantine had few ways of making money[16]. But the Thenardiers kept demanding[17] more money. So Fantine began to sell the only thing she had left, her body.

---

9. **discover** [dɪsˈkʌvər] (v.) 發現
10. **unwed** [ʌnˈwed] (a.) 未結婚的
11. **fire** [faɪr] (v.) 開除；解僱
12. **save** [seɪv] (v.) 存（錢）
13. **sew** [soʊ] (v.) 縫紉
    (sew-sewed-sewn/sewed)
14. **wig-maker** 假髮製造者
15. **medicine** [ˈmedɪsən] (n.) 藥
16. **make money** 賺錢
17. **demand** [dɪˈmænd] (v.) 要求

A Match.

1 Jean Valjean •   • a an old man who always helps everybody in need

2 Fantine •   • b a man who manages a small inn and needs lots of money

3 the Bishop of Digne •   • c a criminal who was in prison for nineteen years

4 Cosette •   • d a young woman who got pregnant by a man who ran away

5 M. Thenardier •   • e the daughter of Fantine

B Rearrange the sentences in chronological order.

1 The Thenardiers wrote a letter that they needed more money to buy medicine for Cosette.

2 Fantine sent the Thenardiers money every month.

3 Fantine lost her job at the factory where she worked.

4 Fantine asked the Thenardiers to take care of her daughter.

5 Fantine began to sell her body.

_____ ⇨ _____ ⇨ _____ ⇨ _____ ⇨ _____

C Choose the correct answer.

1 What did Jean Valjean steal from the Bishop of Digne's house?

(a) Money
(b) Valuable silverware
(c) Two silver candlesticks

2 What was the job of the boy from whom Jean Valjean stole the coin?

(a) He was a police officer.
(b) He was a farmer.
(c) He was a chimney sweep.

D Choose the correct answer.

1 (a) He was <u>desperate</u> for a place to rest.

(b) Even though he was <u>desperate</u>, he woke up only a few hours later.

2 (a) The bishop's sleeping face looked so <u>furious</u> and kind.

(b) Life had been terribly unfair to him, and he was still <u>furious</u> about it.

3 (a) The boy became very <u>frightened</u> and ran away.

(b) Fantine said goodbye to her daughter, crying as if her heart was <u>frightened</u>.

The Guardian[1]

On a cold winter night, a poor-looking woman with no teeth was arrested[2] for attacking[3] a man on the street. At the police station[4], Inspector[5] Javert decided to send her to prison[6] for six months.

"Please don't send me to prison," cried the woman. "If I don't pay the money I owe, my daughter will lose her home and have to live in the streets!"

Inspector Javert ignored[7] her and told his men to take her away. But suddenly a voice said, "Wait just a moment, please. I saw what happened in the street. It was the man's fault, not this woman's."

---

1. **guardian** ['gɑ:rdiən] (n.) 守護者
2. **arrest** [ə'rest] (v.) 逮捕
3. **attack** [ə'tæk] (v.) 攻擊
4. **police station** 警局
5. **inspector** [ɪn'spektər] (n.) 警探
6. **send** *A* **to prison** 將 A 送進牢裡
7. **ignore** [ɪg'nɔ:r] (v.) 忽視
8. **mayor** ['meɪər] (n.) 鎮（市）長
9. **penniless** ['penɪləs] (a.) 身無分文的
10. **method** ['meθəd] (n.) 方法
11. **townspeople** ['taʊnzpi:pəl] (n.) 鎮民
12. **elect** [ɪ'lekt] (v.) 選舉

Javert looked up to see Mayor[8] Madeline, the most important man in town.

Before he was the town's mayor, M. Madeline had arrived suddenly on a winter evening in 1815. He had been penniless[9] but knew of a new method[10] for making glass at a very low cost. Within a few months, his new glass-making factory made him a rich man. With that money, he built two new factories and brought hundreds of jobs to the town.

He lived a simple life and spent most of his money building hospitals and schools. In 1820, the townspeople[11] elected[12] him mayor of the town.

33

But one man in town did not like Mayor Madeline. Inspector Javert was always suspicious of[1] the man who had been a stranger. He felt he had seen the mayor's face before, as if he had been a dangerous criminal at an earlier time.

Now the mayor was in Javert's police station, trying to save Fantine from going to prison. But when Fantine saw the mayor, she spat at[2] him. "You own the factory where I lost my job! Now I've become a bad woman, and I'll never get my daughter back!"

Javert and the mayor argued[3], but Fantine was finally released. Then Mayor Madeline said to her, "I didn't mean to[4] cause[5] all of these troubles for you. I'm going to help you. I'm going to pay your debts and get your daughter back to you. In God's eyes you are not a bad woman."

1. **suspicious of** 對……起疑
2. **spit at** A 朝 A 吐口水
3. **argue** [ˈɑːrgjuː] (v.) 爭執；爭論
4. **mean to** 故意
5. **cause** [kɔːz] (v.) 造成
6. **kneel down** 跪下

Fantine wept at the kindness the mayor was showing her. She knelt down[6] and kissed his hand.

The mayor sent the Thenardiers 300 francs and told them to send Cosette to him right away. But M. Thenardier wrote back, demanding 500 francs. Mayor Madeline sent the money, but the Thenardiers still didn't send Cosette.

Even though Fantine was close to being happy again, the years of misery[1] and poverty[2] had left her very weak[3]. She became very sick and couldn't get out of bed. Whenever Mayor Madeline visited her, all she asked was, "When can I see my Cosette?"

"Soon," he said, to which she would smile with joy[4].

1. **misery** ['mɪzəri] (n.) 悲慘；痛苦
2. **poverty** ['pɑ:vərti] (n.) 窮困
3. **weak** [wiːk] (a.) 虛弱的
4. **with joy** 愉快地
5. **prepare to** 準備做……
6. **pick up** 接（人）
7. **apologize for** 為……道歉

One morning, Mayor Madeline was preparing to[5] travel to the Thenardiers' town himself and pick Cosette up[6]. But Inspector Javert suddenly came into his office.

"I want to apologize for[7] being suspicious of you," said the inspector.

"What are you talking about?" asked Mayor Madeline.

"For years, I've suspected you of being the escaped criminal Jean Valjean. But now, the police in another town have caught the real Jean Valjean. The man says his name is Champmathieu, but there are several witnesses[8] who swear[9] he is Jean Valjean. He will face trial[10] tomorrow and go to prison for life[11]. I am sorry for doubting[12] you."

8. **witness** ['wɪtnɪs] (n.)
   目擊者；證人
9. **swear** [swer] (v.)
   發誓；保證
   (swear-swore-sworn)

10. **trial** ['traɪəl] (n.) 審判
11. **for life** 終生
12. **doubt** [daʊt] (v.) 懷疑

✓ Check Up Fill in the blank with proper word.
Javert visited Valjean to _____ to him for his doubt.

Ans: apologize

🎧 12

The inspector left, and Mayor Madeline canceled[1] his trip to visit the Thenardiers for the following day. That night he lay awake[2] in bed. Mayor Madeline was in fact[3] Jean Valjean. He could not let the man Champmathieu spend the rest of his life in prison for his crimes[4]. He would have to go to the man's trial and admit[5] the truth. He would lose everything he had worked for, but he had no choice. The truth was the most important thing.

The next morning, Mayor Madeline traveled to the town where the trial was taking place[6]. When he arrived, he saw that Champmathieu was a large man-child who was not intelligent[7] enough to defend himself[8]. Just when the judge[9] was about to[10] convict Champmathieu of[11] being Jean Valjean, Mayor Madeline stood up and said, "This man is not Jean Valjean. I am."

1. **cancel** [ˈkænsəl] (v.) 取消
2. **awake** [əˈweɪk] (a.) 清醒的
3. **in fact** 事實上
4. **crime** [kraɪm] (n.) 罪行
5. **admit** [ədˈmɪt] (v.) 承認
6. **take place** 發生
7. **intelligent** [ɪnˈtelɪdʒənt] (a.) 有智慧的；聰明的
8. **defend oneself** 為自己辯護
9. **judge** [dʒʌdʒ] (n.) 法官
10. **be about to** 即將……
11. **convict A of** 因……判決 A

Gasps[12] were heard around the courtroom[13].
No one believed him at first[14]. But he told
them information[15] that only Jean Valjean
could have known.

"I must leave now," said Mayor Madeline.
"I have some business I must do. But I'll not
try to escape when my business is finished."

They let him leave the courtroom, and the
judge allowed Champmathieu to[16] go free.

12. **gasp** [gæsp] (n.)
    （因驚訝等而）倒抽一口氣
13. **courtroom** [ˈkɔːrtruːm]
    (n.) 法庭

14. **at first** 起初
15. **information** [ˌɪnfərˈmeɪʃən]
    (n.) 資訊
16. **allow A to** 允許 A……

The next day, Mayor Madeline visited Fantine. When she saw him, she asked for Cosette.

"Not now. You're too weak to see her. You must get well[1] first," he said.

Then Inspector Javert entered[2] the room. Fantine thought the inspector was there to arrest her and became afraid. But Mayor Madeline said, "He's not here for you." Then to Inspector Javert he said, "Just give me three days to go and get her child, and then you can take me to prison."

"I'm not going to give you three days to escape," said Inspector Javert.

"But my child!" cried Fantine.

"Shut up[3], you dirty whore[4]!" shouted Inspector Javert. "This man is not Mayor Madeline, and he's never going to bring your daughter to you. He is a dangerous criminal named Jean Valjean, and he's going to prison!"

1. **get well** 康復
2. **enter** ['entər] (v.) 進入
3. **shut up** 住口
4. **whore** [hɔːr] (n.) 妓女
5. **fall back** 往後倒
6. **pillow** ['pɪloʊ] (n.) 枕頭
7. **totally** ['toʊtli] (adv.) 完全地
8. **bedside** ['bedsaɪd] (n.) 床邊
9. **yell at** 對……叫喊
10. **by force** 藉由武力

Fantine fell back[5] on her pillow[6] and lay totally[7] still. Jean Valjean ran to her bedside[8]. She was dead. "Your words have killed her!" he yelled at[9] Inspector Javert.

"Come to the police station with me now, or I'll call my men to arrest you by force[10]," said Javert.

Jean Valjean kissed Fantine's head and said to the inspector, "I'm ready to go now."

◆ I'm not **going to give** you three days to escape.
我不會給你三天的時間逃跑的。

be going to + 原形動詞：表示即將……

e.g. I'm **going to visit** my grandmother this summer.
今年暑假我將去拜訪我的祖母。

🎧 14

Two days after being arrested, Jean Valjean escaped from prison. He managed to break the bars[1] over his window and disappeared[2] into the night.

On Christmas in 1823, business at the Thenardiers' inn was very good. The guests ate and drank noisily[3] while Cosette, now eight years old, sat in her normal[4] place under the kitchen table. She was dressed in[5] rags, knitting[6] wool stockings[7] for the Thenardiers' two daughters.

One night, Mme. Thenardier ordered Cosette to[8] go out in the cold to get a bucket of[9] water. As she left, Mme. Thenardier gave her a coin[10] and told her to get some bread, too.

1. **bar** [bɑːr] (n.) 欄杆
2. **disappear** [ˌdɪsəˈpɪr] (v.) 消失
3. **noisily** [ˈnɔɪzili] (adv.) 嘈雜地
4. **normal** [ˈnɔːrməl] (a.) 平常的
5. **be dressed in** 穿著……
6. **knit** [nɪt] (v.) 編織 (knit-knitted-knitted)
7. **wool stockings** 羊毛長襪
8. **order A to** 命令 A 去……
9. **a bucket of** 一桶……
10. **coin** [kɔɪn] (n.) 銅板

Cosette walked through the dark woods[11] to the stream[12]. As she filled[13] her large wooden bucket, she didn't notice the coin Mme. Thenardier had given her fall through a hole[14] in her pocket and into the frigid[15] water.

Then she began to lug[16] the heavy bucket full of[17] water through the woods and up the hill[18] to the inn. The bucket was so heavy that she had to stop every few steps for some rest.

11. **woods** [wʊdz] (n.) 樹林
12. **stream** [stri:m] (n.) 溪
13. **fill** [fɪl] (v.) 裝滿
14. **hole** [hoʊl] (n.) 洞
15. **frigid** [ˈfrɪdʒɪd] (a.) 寒冷的
16. **lug** [lʌg] (v.) 使勁拉
    (lug-lugged-lugged)
17. **full of** 充滿
18. **hill** [hɪl] (n.) 小山丘

Suddenly a huge[1] hand reached down[2] from the sky and picked up the water bucket. Cosette looked up to see an enormous[3] old man standing there.

"What a heavy bucket this must be for a child as small as you," the man said while looking at her through gentle eyes.

Cosette was not afraid of the man. She trusted[4] his eyes. They walked back through the village together. As they walked, she told him everything about her life with the Thenardiers. As they neared[5] the inn, he gave her the bucket, and they entered the inn together.

"Why were you gone so long?" Mme.

1. **huge** [hju:dʒ] (a.) 巨大的
2. **reach down** 往下伸
3. **enormous** [ɪˈnɔ:rməs] (a.) 巨大的
4. **trust** [trʌst] (v.) 信任;相信
5. **near** [nɪr] (v.) 接近
6. **in fear of** 害怕
7. **beating** [ˈbi:tɪŋ] (n.) 捶打
8. **expect** [ɪkˈspekt] (v.) 期待;預期
9. **seat** [si:t] (v.) 使……就座
10. **search** [sɜ:rtʃ] (v.) 尋找
11. **pale** [peɪl] (a.) 蒼白的
12. **hold up** 舉起

Thenardier asked angrily.

"I . . . I met this man who needs a room for the night," Cosette said in fear of[6] the beating[7] she expected[8]. Mme. Thenardier seated[9] the old man with a glass of wine, and then asked Cosette, "Where's the bread I told you to buy?"

"I . . . I forgot to get it, Madame."

"Then where's the money I gave you?"

Cosette searched[10] her pocket, but the coin was not there. She went pale[11]. Then suddenly the old man held up[12] a coin.

"Madame, I've just found this on the floor. It must have fallen from the child's pocket." Mme. Thenardier took the coin and walked away.

✓ Check Up　Choose the correct answer.
The old man helped Cosette with ＿＿ the bucket ＿＿ water.
ⓐ throwing / into　ⓑ pulling / out of　ⓒ carrying / full of

Ans: c

One Point Lesson

◈ She **went pale.** 她的臉變得慘白。

go + 形容詞：轉變成⋯⋯

e.g. He **went mad** after his wife died.
他的妻子過世後，他就瘋了。

16

The next morning, the old man spoke to the Thenardiers. "It seems like[1] you don't have enough money to take care of this child very well. Why don't you let me take her?"

"We love her very much," said M. Thenardier. "We couldn't let you have her for less than[2] 1,500 francs."

The old man quickly handed him three 500-franc notes and said, "Now fetch[3] Cosette."

The man gave her some fine new clothes and they left hand in hand[4] for Paris. Cosette didn't know who the man was, but she had a comforting[5] feeling that God was guarding[6] her through this man. The man was Jean Valjean.

Jean Valjean took Cosette to a large old building on the outskirts of[7] Paris. Cosette was asleep in his arms. He took her up to the room he had rented[8] since his escape from Inspector Javert.

1. **it seems like** 似乎
2. **less than** 少於
3. **fetch** [fetʃ] (v.) 拿來;交出
4. **hand in hand** 手牽手
5. **comforting** [ˈkʌmfərtɪŋ] (a.) 令人欣慰的
6. **guard** [gɑːrd] (v.) 守衛
7. **on the outskirts of** 在……的郊外
8. **rent** [rent] (v.) 租
9. **pass** [pæs] (v.) (時間)流逝

The days began to pass[9] in great
happiness for Cosette and Valjean. For him,
it was the first time in twenty-five years that
he was not alone in the world. His heart had
discovered love.

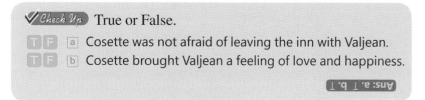

✔ Check Up True or False.

T F a Cosette was not afraid of leaving the inn with Valjean.

T F b Cosette brought Valjean a feeling of love and happiness.

Ans: a.T b.T

One evening, Valjean heard someone on the stairs[1] outside his room. He ran to the keyhole[2] and saw the back of a familiar[3] coat walking down the stairs. "Javert," he said to himself[4].

The next day, he prepared to leave their room for a safer place. That night, as they walked along the narrow streets under the light of the full moon, Valjean realized[5] four men were following them at a distance[6].

As he looked back, through the moonlight, he could clearly see the face of Inspector Javert. He gripped[7] Cosette's hand tightly[8] and began to weave[9] through the confusing[10] system of alleyways[11].

After walking down a long lane[12], he came to a dead end[13]. There was a tall building with barred windows and doors on one side, and a high wall on the other. He could climb the wall himself, but how could he bring Cosette?

---

1. **stairs** [sterz] (n.) 樓梯
2. **keyhole** [ˈkiːhoʊl] (n.) 鑰匙孔
3. **familiar** [fəˈmɪljər] (a.) 熟悉的
4. **say to oneself** 心中暗想
5. **realize** [ˈrɪəlaɪz] (v.) 發現
6. **at a distance** 有相當距離地
7. **grip** [grɪp] (v.) 緊握
8. **tightly** [taɪtli] (adv.) 緊緊地
9. **weave** [wiːv] (v.) 迂迴行進 (weave-wove/weaved-wove/weaved)

Then he noticed a streetlight[14] and had an idea. He opened up the box at its base[15] and ripped out[16] some wires. Then he tied[17] the wire[18] around Cosette's waist[19] and climbed the wall, pulling her up after him. On the other side of the wall was a tree. He lowered[20] Cosette into the tree's branches[21] and leapt[22] over the wall just as the four men got there.

10. **confusing** [kənˈfjuːzɪŋ] (a.) 令人困惑的
11. **alleyway** [ˈæliweɪ] (n.) 小巷
12. **lane** [leɪn] (n.) 小路；巷弄
13. **dead end** 死路
14. **streetlight** [ˈstriːtlaɪt] (n.) 街燈
15. **at one's base** 在底部
16. **rip out** 扯出

17. **tie** [taɪ] (v.) 綁
18. **wire** [waɪr] (n.) 電線
19. **waist** [weɪst] (n.) 腰部
20. **lower** [ˈloʊər] (v.) 放低
21. **branch** [bræntʃ] (n.) 樹枝
22. **leap** [liːp] (v.) 跳（躍）
    (leap-leapt-leapt)

Chapter Two

A True or False.

T F ❶ Mayor Madeline wanted Fantine to go to prison for six months.

T F ❷ Inspector Javert suspected Mayor Madeline of being Jean Valjean.

T F ❸ The Thenardiers treated Cosette as if she were one of their own daughters.

T F ❹ Cosette bought the bread that Mme. Thenardier asked her to buy.

T F ❺ Inspector Javert almost caught Valjean and Cosette in an alleyway in Paris.

B Match.

❶ Mayor Madeline •

❷ M. Thenardier •

❸ Cosette •

❹ Inspector Javert •

❺ Fantine •

• ⓐ If I don't pay the money I owe, my daughter will lose her home and have to live in the streets!

• ⓑ I didn't mean to cause all those troubles for you.

• ⓒ I am sorry for doubting you.

• ⓓ I met this man who needs a room for the night.

• ⓔ We couldn't let you have her for less than 1,500 francs.

C Choose the correct answer.

❶ Why was Champmathieu on trial?

   (a) Because he was a man-child.

   (b) Because he was a friend of Jean Valjean.

   (c) Because he was accused of being the real Jean Valjean.

❷ Where did Valjean and Cosette live after he rescued her from the Thenardiers?

   (a) They lived in a large old building on the outskirts of Paris.

   (b) They lived on a small farm near Paris.

   (c) They lived with the Bishop of Digne.

D Fill in the blanks with the given words.

discovered	escaped	trusted	ignored

❶ Inspector Javert _____ her and told his men to take her away.

❷ Two days after being arrested, Jean Valjean _____ from prison.

❸ Cosette _____ the man's eyes.

❹ Jean Valjean's heart had _____ love.

The Models of
the Characters

Some of the characters in this story are based on[1] people who really lived.

Victor Hugo heard the story of a kindly priest[2] named Miollis, who took in[3] a released convict[4] for the night. When the convict repaid[5] the bishop by stealing his silver dinnerware, Miollis told the police that he gave the valuables[6] to the man. This is just one of the true stories about the priest who later became the Bishop of Digne in 1806. The real man's generosity and kindness became legend in France.

1. **be based on** 根據⋯⋯
2. **priest** [priːst] (n.) 神父
3. **take in** 接受
4. **convict** [kənˈvɪkt] (n.) 囚犯
5. **repay** [rɪˈpeɪ] (v.) 回報
   (repay-repaid-repaid)
6. **valuables** [ˈvæljʊbəlz] (n.) 貴重物品
7. **justice** [ˈdʒʌstɪs] (n.) 公正；正義
8. **prisoner** [ˈprɪzənər] (n.) 犯人
9. **execute** [ˈeksɪkjuːt] (v.)
   將⋯⋯處死
10. **jailer** [ˈdʒeɪlər] (n.) 獄卒
11. **sympathize with** 同情
12. **outcome** [ˈaʊtkʌm] (n.) 結果
13. **include** [ɪnˈkluːd] (v.) 包括
14. **idealistic** [aɪˌdɪəˈlɪstɪk] (a.)
    完美主義的
15. **experience** [ɪkˈspɪriəns]
    (v.) 經歷

The character of Jean Valjean was also based on a real character. Hugo was very interested in social justice[7] and the criminal system in France. He would visit prisons and interview the prisoners[8]. Gueux was one of them. He told Hugo how he had been sent to prison because he broke into a house to steal bread for his children.

Unlike the fictional Jean Valjean, however, Gueux was executed[9] for killing a jailer[10] while in prison. Hugo sympathized with[11] Gueux because the jailer was extremely cruel to Gueux. Hugo felt that Gueux should not have been in prison in the first place. In his work, *Les Misérables*, Hugo wanted to show the entire chain of events that led to punishment–to throw doubt on the justice of the final outcome[12].

Other characters that were taken from real life include[13] Cosette and Marius. Hugo actually based Marius on himself when he was a young idealistic[14] man who experienced[15] love for the first time. His wife is an obvious model for Cosette.

· Chapter Three ·

🎧 18 # The Parisians¹

A night after the Battle² of Waterloo in June 1815, a robber³ quietly stole money and jewelry⁴ from the bodies of dead soldiers⁵ on the battlefield⁶. In the moonlight, he saw a hand with a gold ring on its finger. As he took the ring, the hand grabbed⁷ his jacket. He pulled the body from the pile⁸ of other dead bodies to find a French officer⁹ who was still alive¹⁰.

"Thank you for saving my life. What is your name?" asked the officer.

"Thenardier," replied the robber.

"I'll never forget your name," said the officer. "And you must remember mine. My name is Pontmercy."

---

1. **Parisian** [pəˈrɪʒən] (n.) 巴黎人
2. **battle** [ˈbætl] (n.) 戰役
3. **robber** [ˈrɑːbər] (n.) 強盜
4. **jewelry** [ˈdʒuːəlri] (n.) 珠寶
5. **soldier** [ˈsoʊldʒər] (n.) 士兵
6. **battlefield** [ˈbætlfiːld] (n.) 戰場

Then the robber took the man's watch and wallet and disappeared. The officer, whose name was Georges Pontmercy, had a son named Marius. Marius, whose mother had died, lived with his grandfather, a very wealthy[11] man named M. Gellenormand. But M. Gillenormand hated his son-in-law[12], Marius' father.

After Georges Pontmercy recovered[13] from his injury[14], M. Gillenormand paid him to stay away from[15] his son. Pontmercy accepted[16] the offer[17] because he wanted his son to have a good life.

---

7. **grab** [græb] (v.) 抓取
8. **pile** [paɪl] (n.) 堆；疊
9. **officer** [ˈɒːfɪsər] (n.) 軍官
10. **alive** [əˈlaɪv] (a.) 活著的
11. **wealthy** [ˈwelθi] (a.) 富有的
12. **son-in-law** 女婿
13. **recover** [rɪˈkʌvər] (v.) 康復
14. **injury** [ˈɪndʒəri] (n.) （身體等的）傷害
15. **stay away from** 遠離
16. **accept** [əkˈsept] (v.) 接受
17. **offer** [ˈɑːfər] (n.) 提議

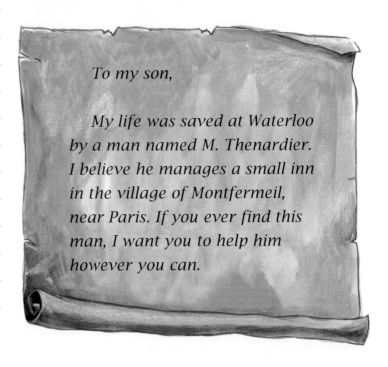

For years, M. Gillenormand told Marius his father was a bad man. But when Marius turned 17, he learned the truth that his father had been a brave soldier. Marius searched for[1] his father, but by the time he found him, he had died. All Marius received[2] from his father was a letter:

> *To my son,*
>
> *My life was saved at Waterloo by a man named M. Thenardier. I believe he manages a small inn in the village of Montfermeil, near Paris. If you ever find this man, I want you to help him however you can.*

1. **search for** 尋找
2. **receive** [rɪ'siːv] (v.) 收到
3. **find out** 找出
4. **grave** [greɪv] (n.) 墓地
5. **argument** ['ɑːrgjʊmənt] (n.) 爭執
6. **coincidentally** [koʊˌɪnsɪ'dentli] (adv.) 巧合地
7. **survive** [sər'vaɪv] (v.) 倖存

When M. Gillenormand found out[3] that Marius was visiting his father's grave[4], they had a big argument[5]. Then M. Gillenormand made Marius leave his house.

For the following three years, Marius lived in a small room in an old building on the outskirts of Paris. Coincidentally[6], it was the same room that Valjean and Cosette had lived in eight years earlier. Marius made little money, but it was enough to survive[7]. His grandfather often tried to send him money, but he refused it. Marius hated his grandfather for the cruel way he had treated his father.

Marius was a handsome young man, but he was very shy. He lived a quiet life of studying, writing, and taking daily walks[1].

Sometimes on his walks, Marius noticed an elderly[2] man and a young girl, who always sat on the same bench in the Luxembourg Gardens[3]. The girl was thirteen or fourteen and always wore the same black dress. But what Marius noticed were her lovely blue eyes.

For some reason, Marius stopped going to the Luxembourg Gardens. When he returned one year later, they were in the same place. The only difference was that the thin girl of a year earlier had become a beautiful young woman. She had soft, brown hair, smooth[4], pale skin, deep, blue eyes, and a gorgeous[5] smile.

One day as he passed, their eyes met, and he felt that his life would never be the same. He began to watch the old man and the girl every day. He followed them so much that the old man started to become suspicious of him and began coming to the gardens less frequently, sometimes without the girl.

When the old man and girl stopped visiting[6] the gardens, Marius became depressed[7]. So he tried to find out where they lived. Finally, he learned they lived in a small house at the end of a street named Rue de l'Quest.

1. **take a walk** 散步
2. **elderly** ['eldərli] (a.) 年長的
3. **gardens** ['gɑːrdns] (n.)
   〔複〕（公有的）公園
4. **smooth** [smuːð] (a.) 平滑的
5. **gorgeous** ['gɔːrdʒəs] (a.) 燦爛的
6. **stop+***V-ing* 停止（動作）
7. **depressed** [dɪ'prest] (a.) 沮喪的

Marius began to follow them home and watch them through their lighted[1] window. When he caught a glimpse of[2] the girl, his heart began to beat[3] faster. On the eighth night of coming to the house, the lights in the windows were out. When he saw this, he knocked on[4] their neighbor's door and asked where they were.

"They've moved out[5]," said the neighbor. Then the neighbor slammed[6] the door in Marius' face.

Summer and fall passed, and Marius did not see the old man or the young girl whom he had fallen in love with[7]. Depressed, he wandered the streets like a lost puppy. Without the young woman, life seemed meaningless[8] to him.

Then one day, Marius found a packet of[9] four letters near his room. When he read the letters, he saw that they were supposedly[10] written by four different people. Yet they were all written by the same hand. They stank of[11] cheap tobacco[12], and they were all asking for money.

---

1. **lighted** ['laɪtɪd] (a.) 有光的
2. **catch a glimpse of** 瞥見
3. **beat** [biːt] (v.) 跳動
   (beat-beat-beaten)
4. **knock on** 敲（門）
5. **move out** 搬出

6. **slam** [slæm] (v.) 猛地關上
   (slam-slammed-slammed)
7. **fall in love with** 愛上
8. **meaningless** ['miːnɪŋləs] (a.)
   無意義的
9. **a packet of** 一包……

The next morning, there was a knock on Marius' door. When he opened it, he saw a thin, sick-looking girl who was missing[13] some teeth. She was his next-door[14] neighbor's daughter. She gave him a letter from her father:

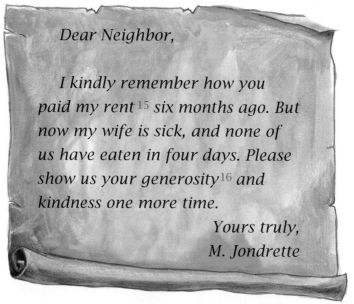

Dear Neighbor,

I kindly remember how you paid my rent[15] six months ago. But now my wife is sick, and none of us have eaten in four days. Please show us your generosity[16] and kindness one more time.

Yours truly,
M. Jondrette

✔ *Check Up*

The letter from Marius' neighbor begged for _____.

  [a] love   [b] money   [c] forgiveness   Ans: b

10. **supposedly** [sə'poʊzɪdli]
    (adv.) 大概；可能
11. **stink of . . .** 發出……的惡臭
    (stink-stank-stunk)
12. **tobacco** [tə'bækoʊ] (n.) 菸草
13. **miss** [mɪs] (v.) 失去
14. **next-door** 隔壁的
15. **rent** [rent] (n.) 租金
16. **generosity** [ˌdʒenə'rɑːsəti]
    (n.) 慷慨

Marius realized that the handwriting[1] and cheap tobacco smell was the same as the letters he had found the night before. All of them were from the poor family in the next room. He had never paid attention to[2] the Jondrettes in the months they had been his neighbors. But now he realized M. Jondrette's business was writing dishonest[3] letters that asked for money from people who he thought were wealthier than him.

1. **handwriting** ['hænd,raɪtɪŋ] (n.) 筆跡
2. **pay attention to** 注意
3. **dishonest** [dɪs'ɑːnɪst] (a.) 不誠實的
4. **shoulder** ['ʃoʊldər] (n.) 肩膀
5. **all the time** 一直；始終
6. **move away from** 移開
7. **touch** [tʌtʃ] (n.) 碰觸
8. **parcel** ['pɑːrsəl] (n.) 包裹
9. **all over** 到處
10. **take out** 拿出

While Marius was reading the letter, the girl watched him. Then she moved closer to him and put her cold hand on his shoulder[4].

"You know, Monsieur Marius, you're a very handsome boy. You never notice me, but I see you looking lonely all the time[5]."

"I think I have something of yours," Marius said, moving away from[6] her touch[7]. He handed her the parcel[8] of four letters that he had found.

"Oh yes, I've been looking all over[9] for these." Taking out[10] one of the letters, she said, "This one is for the old man who goes to church every day. If I hurry, I'll be able to catch him on the street. He might give me enough for dinner."

One Point Lesson

If I hurry, I'll be able to catch him on the street.
如果我快一點的話，就可以在街上堵到他。

will be able to + 原形動詞：表示能夠做某件事，或可以進行某個動作

e.g He will be able to start his own business next year.
他明年就能開始自己的事業了。

23

Marius took a coin from his pocket and handed it to the girl.

"Ah-ha!" she cried, "That's enough money to eat for two days! You're an angel[1], Monsieur Marius." Then she laughed, grabbed a piece of dried[2] bread from Marius' table, and left.

Marius realized that although he lived on[3] little money, he had not known what it meant to be poor until he had become acquainted with this miserable[4] family in the next room. As he was thinking about this desperate family, he noticed a small triangular[5] hole in the corner of the wall that separated his room from theirs[6]. He decided to observe[7] them.

1. **angel** [ˈeɪndʒəl] (n.) 天使
2. **dried** [draɪd] (a.) 乾掉的
3. **live on** 靠……生活
4. **miserable** [ˈmɪzərəbəl] (a.) 不幸的；悲慘的
5. **triangular** [traɪˈæŋgjʊlər] (a.) 三角形的
6. **separate** *A* **from** *B* 將 A 與 B 區隔開
7. **observe** [əbˈzɜːrv] (v.) 觀察
8. **cupboard** [ˈkʌbərd] (n.) 櫥櫃
9. **filthy** [ˈfɪlθi] (a.) 髒亂的
10. **foul-smelling** 臭氣沖天的
11. **bare** [ber] (a.) 無陳設的；光禿禿的

Marius stood on a cupboard[8] and put his eye to the hole. The Jondrettes' room was filthy[9] and foul-smelling[10], unlike Marius' bare[11], clean dwelling[12]. The only furniture[13] was a broken table, a chair, and two dirty beds. There were a few cracked[14] plates[15] on the table.

There an old man sat, smoking a pipe and writing a letter. A large woman with graying[16] hair that was once red sat next to the fireplace[17], and a thin, sickly-looking girl sat on one of the beds. Marius was depressed by what he saw.

12. **dwelling** ['dwelɪŋ] (n.) 住處
13. **furniture** ['fɜːrnɪtʃər] (n.) 家具
14. **cracked** [krækt] (a.) 破裂的
15. **plate** [pleɪt] (n.) 盤子
16. **graying** ['greɪɪŋ] (a.) 灰白的
17. **fireplace** ['faɪrpleɪs] (n.) 壁爐

24

Marius was going to stop looking, when suddenly the girl who had come to his room bounded[1] through the Jondrettes' door.

"He's coming," she cried happily.

"Who's coming?" asked the father.

"The old man who goes to church with his daughter every day. I saw them on the street, and he's coming. I ran ahead[2] to tell you. They'll be here in two minutes.

"Good girl," said M. Jondrette. "Quickly! Put out[3] the fire!"

1. **bound** [baʊnd] (v.) 跳起
2. **ahead** [əˈhed] (adv.) 預先；在前
3. **put out** 熄滅
4. **pour** [pɔːr] (v.) 倒；灌
5. **fist** [fɪst] (n.) 拳頭
6. **badly** [ˈbædli] (adv.) 嚴重地
7. **covered in** 被……覆蓋
8. **blood** [blʌd] (n.) 血
9. **bow** [baʊ] (v.) 鞠躬
10. **in shock** 震驚的

The girl poured⁴ water on the fire while M. Jondrette broke the chair with his foot. He told his younger daughter to break the window. The girl put her fist⁵ through the glass and cut her arm very badly⁶. She ran to the bed covered in⁷ blood⁸.

"Great, the more miserable we look, the more money the kind gentleman will give us."

Then there came a knock at the door. M. Jondrette opened the door, bowing⁹ almost to the floor. The old man and the young girl entered the room.

Marius was in shock¹⁰. It was the old man from the park! It was the young girl he had fallen in love with!

One Point Lesson

Great, **the more miserable** we look, **the more** money the kind gentleman will give us.
太好了，我們看起來愈慘，那位善良的紳士就會給我們愈多錢。

the + 比較級 , the + 比較級：愈……愈……

e.g. **The sooner, the better.** 愈快愈好。

25

The old man handed M. Jondrette a package. "Here are some warm clothes and blankets[1] for your family."

"Thank you, sir. As you can see, we are without food or heat. My wife is very sick, and my daughter injured[2] her arm at the factory where she works."

1. **blanket** ['blæŋkɪt] (n.) 毯子
2. **injure** ['ɪndʒər] (v.) 傷害
3. **scream** [skri:m] (v.) 尖叫
4. **pain** [peɪn] (n.) 痛苦
5. **annoyed with** 對⋯⋯感到生氣
6. **suggestive** [səg'dʒestɪv] (a.) 挑逗的；暗示的
7. **in a . . . manner** 以⋯⋯的方式
8. **for a moment** 一會兒
9. **address** ['ædres] (n.) 地址
10. **disappointed** [ˌdɪsə'pɔɪntɪd] (a.) 失望的

The young girl who had hurt her arm screamed[3] with pain[4]. The kind old man took a coin from his pocket and put it on the table.

"Five francs is all I have right now. I'll come back later this evening with some more money for you."

After they left, Marius tried to leave his room to follow them. He had to know where the beautiful young girl lived. But the Jondrette girl was back at his door. She came into his room.

"What do you want?" he asked, annoyed with[5] her.

"You were kind to us this morning. Now I want to be kind to you," she said in a very suggestive[6] manner[7]. "I want to do something for you."

Marius thought for a moment[8].

"Do you know the address[9] of the old man and girl who just visited your home?"

She looked disappointed[10], but said, "No, but I can find out if you wish."

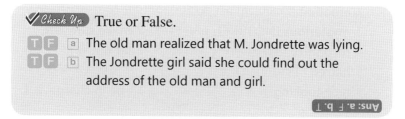

✓ Check Up True or False.

T F a The old man realized that M. Jondrette was lying.
T F b The Jondrette girl said she could find out the address of the old man and girl.

Ans: a. F b. T

🎧 26

The Jondrette girl left, and Marius found himself overcome by[1] emotion[2] for the mysterious[3] young girl. Then he heard M. Jondrette's voice coming through the hole in the wall. He jumped back on the cupboard and listened.

"Are you sure it was them?" asked Mme. Jondrette.

"I'm sure I recognized[4] both of them. It's been eight years, but I'm sure."

"Her?" said Mme. Jondrette. Her voice was filled with hatred[5]. "You must be wrong. That child was ugly, but this girl is nice-looking[6]."

"I'm telling you, she's the same one," said M. Jondrette. "And they're going to bring us lots of money again! When that old man comes back at six o'clock, I'll have a gang of[7] friends here to make sure[8] he gives us all of his money, or he won't leave this room walking on two legs." Then M. Jondrette let out[9] an ugly laugh.

1. **overcome by** 被……壓倒
2. **emotion** [ɪˈmoʊʃən] (n.) 感情
3. **mysterious** [mɪˈstɪriəs] (a.) 神秘的
4. **recognize** [ˈrɛkəgnaɪz] (v.) 認出
5. **hatred** [ˈheɪtrɪd] (n.) 憎恨
6. **nice-looking** 好看的；漂亮的
7. **a gang of** 一群……；一幫……
8. **make sure** 確定
9. **let out** 發出（叫喊或笑聲等）
10. **be in charge** 負責

Marius knew he had to save the old man and the young girl he loved. He went to the nearest police station and asked to speak to the chief.

"He's away," said a policeman. "I'm the next-in-charge[10]. My name is Inspector Javert. What do you want?"

Marius told the inspector about Jondrette's diabolical[1] plan. When Javert heard the address, his eyes lit up[2]. He gave Marius a small gun[3].

"When you hear trouble starting, shoot[4] this out your window. I'll be nearby, waiting for[5] this signal[6] to come in with my men."

Back in his room, Marius waited nervously[7]. On the other side of the wall, M. Jondrette readied a metal[8] bar in the fire and a long, sharp knife. He put a rope ladder[9] out his window in case[10] they needed to make a quick escape.

At exactly six o'clock, the door opened, and the old man entered. He put four coins on the table. "That is for your rent and food. Now, what else do you need?"

After a few minutes of small talk, M. Jondrette called in his friends. Three men armed with[11] metal poles[12] rushed into[13] the room. The old man picked up the broken chair, ready to fight. Marius prepared to fire his pistol.

"Don't you recognize me?" M. Jondrette asked the old man.

"No," the old man replied.

"My real name isn't Jondrette. It's Thenardier. Now do you know me?"

The old man trembled.

1. **diabolical** [ˌdaɪəˈbɑːlɪkəl] (a.) 殘酷的
2. **light up** 亮起來
3. **gun** [gʌn] (n.) 手槍
4. **shoot** [ˈʃuːt] (v.) 開（槍）；射擊 (shoot-shot-shot)
5. **wait for** 等待
6. **signal** [ˈsɪgnəl] (n.) 信號；暗號
7. **nervously** [ˈnɜːrvəsli] (adv.) 緊張地
8. **metal** [ˈmetl] (a.) 金屬的
9. **rope ladder** 繩梯
10. **in case** 萬一
11. **armed with** 裝備著……
12. **pole** [poʊl] (n.) 竿；棒
13. **rush into** 衝入

🎧 28

Upon hearing[1] the name "Thenardier", Marius almost fell from the cupboard he was standing on. It was the name of the man who had saved his father's life. Suddenly, he could not fire the gun to call the detectives[2] as he had planned.

"Eight years ago, you took Cosette away from us. She was bringing us lots of money. You're the cause of all our problems."

"You're just a dirty criminal," said the old man.

"You think I'm a criminal? I saved an officer's life at the Battle of Waterloo! I'm going to teach you a lesson!"

1. **upon+V-ing** 一……就……
2. **detective** [dɪ'tektɪv] (n.) 探員
3. **pull out** 拔出
4. **burst open** 猛然打開
5. **amid** [ə'mɪd] (prep.) 在……之中
6. **confusion** [kən'fju:ʒən] (n.) 混亂;騷動
7. **missing** ['mɪsɪŋ] (a.) 不見的

The old man tried to jump out the window, but the three men held him down. Marius did not know what to do. Thenardier pulled out[3] his long knife. He was preparing to kill the old man.

But suddenly the door burst open[4], and Inspector Javert appeared with fifteen policemen. They began to arrest everybody in the room. Amid[5] the confusion[6], the old man managed to escape out of the window. He was gone before they noticed him missing[7].

✓ Check Up Fill in the blanks with proper words.
The name "Thenardier" kept Marius from

_____ _____ _____ .

Ans: firing the gun

A Rearrange the sentences in chronological order.

❶ M. Thenardier pulled out a long knife and prepared to kill the old man.

❷ The old man came back at 6 o'clock with more money.

❸ Inspector Javert burst into the room with fifteen police officers.

❹ Marius was shocked when M. Jondrette said his real name was Thenardier.

❺ The old man escaped out of the window.

_____ ⇨ _____ ⇨ _____ ⇨ _____ ⇨ _____

B Choose the correct answer.

❶ (a) The letters <u>stank</u> of cheap tobacco.

(b) M. Thenardier prepared to <u>stank</u> the old man with his knife.

❷ (a) Marius <u>accepted</u> a big argument with his grandfather.

(b) Pontmercy <u>accepted</u> the offer because he wanted his son to have a good life.

C Choose the correct answer.

1 What did Inspector Javert tell Marius to do when he heard trouble starting?

(a) Call the police.
(b) Shoot the gun out his window.
(c) Go into the room and fight the bad men.

2 Where did Marius often see the old man and the young girl?

(a) In his apartment building
(b) At the police station
(c) At the Luxembourg Gardens

D Match.

1 Georges Pontmercy •
2 M. Jondrette •
3 Marius •
4 M. Gillenormand •

• ⓐ His business was writing dishonest letters.
• ⓑ He was a shy, handsome young man.
• ⓒ He hated his son-in-law, Marius' father.
• ⓓ He was an officer who was injured at the Battle of Waterloo.

Chapter Four

The Lovers & Revolution[1]

Marius did not want to give evidence[2] against Thenardier out of respect[3] for his father's wish. Marius moved out of his room and in with his friend Enjolras.

One day, Marius was sitting by a stream, dreaming of[4] his love, when he heard a familiar voice. He looked up and recognized Eponine, the Thenardier's daughter.

"Finally, I've found you," she said. "I've looked everywhere."

Marius said nothing to her.

"You don't seem happy to see me," she said. "But I can make you happy if I want to."

1. **revolution** [ˌrevəˈluːʃən] (n.) 革命
2. **evidence** [ˈevɪdəns] (n.) 證據
3. **respect** [rɪˈspɛkt] (n.) 尊重
4. **dream of** 做夢；夢想著
5. **skip** [skɪp] (v.) 跳 (skip-skipped-skipped)
6. **a bit** 有點
7. **jump up** 跳起
8. **at once** 立刻；馬上
9. **back street** 小街；偏僻巷道
10. **tiny** [ˈtaɪni] (a.) 微小的
11. **wild** [waɪld] (a.) 荒涼的
12. **footstep** [ˈfʊtstep] (n.) 臺階
13. **take a look** 看一下
14. **empty** [ˈempti] (a.) 空的

"How?"

"I've got the address you wanted."

His heart skipped[5] a bit[6]. He jumped up[7] and grabbed her hand.

"Let's go at once[8]!" he cried. "And promise you'll never tell your father the address!"

That night Cosette was alone in the house Jean Valjean had bought a year before. It was a small house on a back street[9] with a tiny[10], wild[11] garden. Valjean was away on business, and she was playing the piano when she heard footsteps[12] in the garden. When she took a look[13], the garden was empty[14].

🎧 30

The following morning, Cosette found a stone lying on a nearby bench. When she picked it up, she could see an envelope[1] that contained[2] a small notebook filled with love poems[3]. She read them over and over[4] and enjoyed everything about the poems. She remembered the handsome young man who was always looking at her in the Luxembourg Gardens, and she knew that these poems were from him.

That night Cosette put on[5] her best dress and made her hair look beautiful. Then she went into the garden and waited. Suddenly she felt she was being watched. It was he! His body was thinner, and his skin was paler than she remembered. But it was he.

"Forgive[6] me for following you for so long. But ever since that day you looked at me in the gardens, I've been lost without you," said the young man.

1. **envelope** [ˈenvəloʊp] (n.) 信封
2. **contain** [kənˈteɪn] (v.) 含有
3. **poem** [ˈpoʊɪm] (n.) 詩
4. **over and over** 反覆；一再
5. **put on** 穿上
6. **forgive** [fərˈgɪv] (v.) 原諒 (forgive-forgave-forgiven)
7. **swoon** [swuːn] (v.) 昏厥；狂喜
8. **backward** [ˈbækwərd] (adv.) 向後地
9. **beneath** [bɪˈniːθ] (prep.) 在……之下
10. **overhead** [ˌoʊvərˈhed] (adv.) 在頭頂上

Cosette was so overcome by his words that she swooned[7] and fell backward[8]. He caught her and held her tightly in his arms.

"Do you love me, too?" he asked her.

"Of course I do," she said. "You know I do."

Then they kissed and sat beneath[9] the blanket of stars overhead[10].

During the month of May 1832, Cosette and Marius met every day in the garden of that hidden[1] little house. All day[2] they would hold hands and stare into[3] each other's eyes. Marius was beginning to think he had gone mad[4] with happiness.

On a beautiful, star-filled evening, Marius found a very unhappy Cosette sitting in the garden.

---

1. **hidden** ['hɪdn] (a.) 隱蔽的
2. **all day** 整天
3. **stare into** 凝視
4. **go mad** 發瘋

5. **say to** 吩咐
6. **pack** [pæk] (v.) 打包
7. **coldly** ['koʊldli] (adv.) 冷漠地
8. **no later than** 不晚於；不遲於

"What's wrong?" Marius asked.

"My father says we may have to move again. He said to⁵ pack⁶ everything and be ready to go to England in a week."

"Will you go with him?" Marius asked her coldly⁷.

"What else can I do?"

"You're going to leave me."

"Oh Marius, don't be so cruel," she said. "You could come, too."

"But I'm poor," he cried. "You need money to go to England. But I have an idea. I won't be here tomorrow."

"Why not?" Cosette cried. "What are you going to do?"

"Don't worry. I'll be back the day after tomorrow. I'll meet you here no later than⁸ 9 p.m. I promise."

One Point Lesson

All day they would hold hands and stare into each other's eyes.
他們整天都握著對方的手，凝視著彼此的眼睛。

would：總是，表過去的習慣

e.g I would play with my brother in the forest.
我和弟弟總在森林裡玩耍。

Marius' grandfather, M. Gillenormand, was
now ninety years old. He was very unhappy
that he had not seen his grandson for years.
He was too proud to admit he was wrong, but
he secretly hoped his beloved[1] grandson would
return one day.

It was a June evening when M. Gillenormand
was staring into the fire, thinking sad
thoughts[2] about Marius. Suddenly a servant
appeared[3] and asked, "Sir, will you accept a
visit from Monsieur Marius?"

1. **beloved** [bɪˈlʌvɪd] (a.) 心愛的
2. **thought** [θɔːt] (n.) 想法
3. **appear** [əˈpɪr] (v.) 出現
4. **shudder** [ˈʃʌdər] (v.) 顫慄
5. **hold back** 抑制
6. **frustration** [frʌˈstreɪʃən] (n.) 無奈;沮喪
7. **blessing** [ˈblesɪŋ] (n.) 祝福

The old man shuddered[4] for a moment and then in a quiet voice, said, "Show him in."

When the young man entered, he asked, "Why are you here? Have you come to apologize to me?"

"No sir," Marius said, holding back[5] his frustration[6]. "I've come to ask you for your blessing[7] of my marriage[8]."

"So you're twenty-one and want to get married[9]. How much money are you currently[10] making?"

"Nothing."

"Then the girl must have money."

"I don't know."

"Twenty-one with no job and no money. Your wife will have to count[11] her change carefully when she goes to the market."

"Please, Grandfather! I love her so much! I beg you to[12] bless[13] us!"

The old man gave a disgusted[14] laugh. "Never!"

---

8. **marriage** ['mærɪdʒ] (n.) 婚姻
9. **get married** 結婚
10. **currently** ['kɜ:rəntli] (adv.) 現在；目前
11. **count** [kaʊnt] (v.) 數；計算

12. **beg** *A* **to** 懇求 A 做……
13. **bless** [bles] (v.) 為……祝福
14. **disgusted** [dɪs'gʌstɪd] (a.) 厭惡的

33

Marius was depressed and exhausted[1]. When he returned to Enjolras' apartment, Enjolras was there with some of his revolutionary[2] friends. The group was excited because there was about to be a battle in the streets between the government[3] soldiers and the revolutionaries.

After they left, Marius took out the gun Inspector Javert had given him in February. He put it in his pocket and wandered around the streets. At nine o'clock, he climbed into her garden, but she was not there as she had promised. There were no lights on in the house, and the windows were closed. Marius was so upset[4] that he beat his fists on the wall.

When he had no more energy left, he sat down. "She was gone[5]," he told himself. There was nothing left for him to do but die.

1. **exhausted** [ɪgˈzɑːstɪd] (a.) 筋疲力盡的
2. **revolutionary** [ˌrevəˈluːʃəneri] (a.) 革命的
3. **government** [ˈgʌvərnmənt] (n.) 政府
4. **upset** [ʌpˈset] (a.) 苦惱的；心煩的
5. **be gone** 離開；不見
6. **barricade** [ˈbærɪˌkeɪd] (n.) 路障
7. **figure** [ˈfɪgjər] (n.) 人影
8. **run off** 跑掉
9. **shadow** [ˈʃædoʊ] (n.) 陰暗處

Then he heard a voice calling his name from the street, "Monsieur Marius!"

"What is it?" he replied.

"Monsieur Marius, your friends are waiting for you at the barricade[6] in the Rue de Chanvrerie. They'll be fighting the soldiers soon."

When Marius looked over the wall, he saw the figure[7] of the Thenardier's daughter, Eponine, running off[8] into the shadows[9].

34

The spring of 1832 found Paris in a state[1] of revolution. When the despotic[2] Charles X was overthrown[3] by a peaceful revolution in 1830, King Louis-Phillipe assumed[4] the throne[5]. The new leader failed to understand the needs[6] and power of the poor and the concept[7] of free speech[8]. He often sent soldiers to attack citizens who were protesting[9] in public[10].

The mood of the workers and the poor was inflamed[11]. When General Lamarque died, their dissatisfaction[12] erupted[13]. General Lamarque had been popular with the French people because he was a staunch[14] supporter[15] of democracy[16] and Napoleon.

The funeral[17] began quietly, but when the large crowd of protesters tried to take the coffin[18] away from the soldiers, shots were fired, and people began to die. Paris was gripped[19] in a state of war.

1. **state** [steɪt] (n.) 狀態
2. **despotic** [deˈspɑ:tɪk] (a.) 專橫的
3. **overthrow** [ˌoʊvərˈθroʊ] (v.) 推翻 (overthrow-overthrew-overthrown)
4. **assume** [əˈsu:m] (v.) 取得
5. **throne** [θroʊn] (n.) 王位
6. **needs** [ni:dz] (n.) 〔複〕需求
7. **concept** [ˈkɑ:nsept] (n.) 概念
8. **speech** [spi:tʃ] (n.) 言論
9. **protest** [prəˈtest] (v.) 抗議
10. **in public** 公開地

Enjolras and his friends were building a barricade outside a wine shop in the market district[20]. As they worked, a tall, gray-haired stranger joined them. Some boys joined their efforts[21] as well. One of them was Eponine, who dressed as a boy so that she would be allowed to stay and help in their struggle[22].

11. **inflame** [ɪnˈfleɪm] (v.)
使憤怒；加劇

12. **dissatisfaction**
[dɪˌsætɪsˈfækʃən] (n.) 不滿

13. **erupt** [ɪˈrʌpt] (v.) 爆發

14. **staunch** [stɑːntʃ] (a.)
堅定的

15. **supporter** [səˈpɔːrtər] (n.)
支持者

16. **democracy** [dɪˈmɑːkrəsi] (n.)
民主制度

17. **funeral** [ˈfjuːnərəl] (n.) 喪禮

18. **coffin** [ˈkɑːfɪn] (n.) 棺木

19. **grip** [grɪp] (v.) 使陷於

20. **district** [ˈdɪstrɪkt] (n.) 區域

21. **effort** [ˈefərt] (n.) 努力

22. **struggle** [ˈstrʌgəl] (n.) 奮鬥

35

When they had finished building the barricade, Enjolras and his men took a rest. There were fifty of them preparing to fight against sixty thousand soldiers. The odds[1] were against them, and they knew it.

As they sat drinking their wine, Enjolras began to suspect[2] the tall, gray-haired stranger of being a spy[3]. "You're a police officer sent here to spy on[4] us. Admit it!" said Enjolras.

The man tried to deny[5] it. But eventually[6] he admitted the truth. He was a police spy.

"My name is Javert," said the man.

Enjolras took him prisoner[7] and tied him to a post[8]. Then he told him, "We are going to shoot you two minutes before the barricade falls."

As Marius neared the barricade, the soldiers attacked.

1. **odds** [ɑːds] (n.) 成功的機率
2. **suspect** [səˈspekt] (v.) 懷疑
3. **spy** [spaɪ] (n.) 間諜
4. **spy on** 刺探；暗中監視
5. **deny** [dɪˈnaɪ] (v.) 否認
6. **eventually** [ɪˈventʃuəli] (adv.) 最後地；終於
7. **take** *A* **prisoner** 將 A 俘虜
8. **post** [poʊst] (n.) 柱；杆
9. **bullet** [ˈbʊlɪt] (n.) 子彈
10. **whizz (= whiz)** [wɪz] (v.) 颼颼掠過
11. **aim a gun at** 舉槍瞄準
12. **rebel** [ˈrebəl] (n.) 反抗者；造反者

Bullets[9] whizzed[10] everywhere. Marius saw Enjolras being attacked by a soldier. He pulled the gun from his pocket and killed the soldier. But while he was saving Enjolras, he did not see another soldier aiming a gun at[11] him. The soldier fired, and at that moment, a boy jumped in front of the gun to save Marius. All around were the dead bodies of rebels[12] and soldiers.

✓ *Check Up* True or False.

T F a Javert admitted that he was a spy of the government soldiers.

T F b Marius was shot while he was saving his friend.

Ans: a. T b. F

36

After battling for some time, the soldiers took control of[1] the top part of the barricade wall. Then everyone heard a voice say, "Get back[2], or I'll blow up[3] this barrel[4] of gunpowder[5], and we'll all die!" It was Marius. He lowered his torch[6] to the barrel, and all the soldiers retreated[7].

Enjolras was overjoyed[8] to see Marius, and they embraced[9]. Then Marius heard a weak voice call his name. He looked down and saw Eponine, dressed in the clothing of a boy and covered in blood.

"Don't worry," he said to her, "We'll get a doctor to help you!"

"No, it's too late," she said as the blood flowed[10] from her

1. **take control of** 控制
2. **get back** 後退
3. **blow up** 炸毀
4. **barrel** [ˈbærəl] (n.) 桶
5. **gunpowder** [ˈɡʌnˌpaʊdər] (n.) 火藥
6. **torch** [tɔːrtʃ] (n.) 火把
7. **retreat** [rɪˈtriːt] (v.) 撤退
8. **overjoyed** [ˌoʊvərˈdʒɔɪd] (a.) 狂喜的
9. **embrace** [ɪmˈbreɪs] (v.) 擁抱
10. **flow** [floʊ] (v.) （水等液體）流動
11. **forehead** [ˈfɔːrhed] (n.) 額頭
12. **be jealous of** 嫉妒

like red wine. She put her head on his knee and asked him to kiss her forehead[11] after she died. Marius said he would.

Then she said, "I can't lie to you. I have a letter in my pocket that Cosette asked me to give you. I was going to keep it since I am so jealous of[12] her. I am in love with you."

Then she died, and Marius kissed her forehead. He read the letter from Cosette:

> *My dear,*
>
> *We must leave this house now. We're going to number 7 Rue de'l' Homme-Arme tonight. In a week we'll move to England. I hope I see you again.*
>
> *All of my love,*
> *Cosette, June 4th*

One Point Lesson

◆ I was going to keep it **since** I am so jealous of her.
因為我嫉妒她，所以本來想要把它 (信) 扣留下來的。

---

since：因為；自……時候起

◆ I couldn't attend the party **since** I was sick.
我無法出席那場派對，因為我生病了。

37

Marius kissed the letter. He still thought he would die on this evening of revolution, but he decided he must send her one last letter. He pulled out[1] his notebook and wrote:

Dearest Cosette,

Our marriage is impossible. My grandfather has refused to give his blessing. I tried to see you, but you were gone. The situation[2] here is very bad. I shall die tonight. I love you eternally[3], and my soul will always be near you.

Love always,
Marius

Then he folded[4] the letter and wrote her address on it. A small boy was passing by[5], and Marius told him to take the letter to the address quickly. The boy took the letter and ran off into the darkness.

Jean Valjean was very upset. He and Cosette had argued for the first time[6] ever. She had not wanted to move out of the house. Now in their new house they went to bed without speaking to each other.

The next day, Valjean heard about the fighting in the city. But he did not care. He was happy that they would soon be in England. But then something caught his eye[7]. In the mirror he could see the blotter[8] that Cosette had used to dry the ink on a letter she had written. He began to read it and realized that she was in love with someone.

1. **pull out** 拔出；拉出
2. **situation** [ˌsɪtʃuˈeɪʃən] (n.) 情勢
3. **eternally** [ɪˈtɜːrnəli] (adv.) 永恆地
4. **fold** [foʊld] (v.) 折疊
5. **pass by** 經過；路過
6. **for the first time** 第一次
7. **catch one's eye** 吸引某人的目光
8. **blotter** [ˈblɑːtər] (n.) 吸墨紙

38

Jean Valjean felt angry and betrayed[1] that someone wanted to take away the only person he had ever loved. He knew that it must be the young man they had seen so often at the Luxembourg Gardens. He went out on the front step[2], his heart burning[3] with hatred.

1. **betrayed** [bɪˈtreɪd] (a.) 被背叛的
2. **front step** 前面的台階
3. **burn** [bɜːrn] (v.) 燃燒 (burn-burnt/burned-burnt/burned)
4. **take revenge on** 報復
5. **National Guard** 國民警衛隊
6. **loaded** [loʊdɪd] (a.) 裝彈藥的
7. **disguise** [dɪsˈgaɪz] (n.) 偽裝

Valjean was wondering how he could take revenge on[4] this man, when a small boy approached with a letter for Cosette. He took the letter and read it. The words, "I shall die tonight," made him happy. The man's death would solve his problem. Perhaps the man was already dead.

Then Valjean realized that he would have to try to save this man for Cosette's happiness even though he hated this man more than anyone in the world.

Thirty minutes later, Valjean put on his old National Guard[5] uniform, stuffed a loaded[6] gun in his pocket, and left for the market district of Paris.

That night, thirty-seven rebels survived behind the barricade. When they collected the dead, they found four National Guardsman uniforms. These uniforms could be used as disguises[7] for the married men in their group.

Check Up Fill in the blanks with proper words.
Valjean decided to _____ Marius for Cosette's _____.

Ans: save, happiness

97

39

The men began to argue about who would stay behind to fight since there were five married men and only four uniforms. Each man wanted to be the one to make the sacrifice[1]. Then a fifth National Guardsman uniform fell in front of them. It was Valjean's. "Now all five men can leave," he said. He joined the group behind the barricade. Shortly after, the soldiers began firing cannonballs[2] at them. The barricade began to crumble[3] under the attack.

As the fighting began, Valjean asked Enjolras if he could be the one to execute[4] Inspector Javert. Enjolras said, "You deserve[5] a reward[6] for giving us that uniform, so yes. Take him in back of the alley[7], and shoot him."

Valjean took Javert back to the alley. On a nearby pile of corpses[8] was the dead body of Eponine. "I think I know that girl," Javert said, sadly resigned to his fate[9]. "Now take your revenge."

---

1. **make a sacrifice** 犧牲
2. **cannonball** [ˈkænənbɑːl] (n.) 砲彈
3. **crumble** [ˈkrʌmbəl] (v.) 摧毀；破壞
4. **execute** [ˈeksɪkjuːt] (v.) 將……處死
5. **deserve** [dɪˈzɜːrv] (v.) 應得
6. **reward** [rɪˈwɔːrd] (n.) 獎賞
7. **alley** [ˈæli] (n.) 小巷

Valjean pulled out his gun and fired it into the air. Then he took out his knife and cut the rope binding[10] Javert's wrists[11]. "You are free to[12] go," he said.

"This is embarrassing[13]," said Javert. "I'd rather you just kill me."

8. **corpse** [kɔːrps] (n.) 屍體
9. **resigned to one's fate**
   聽天由命
10. **bind** [baɪnd] (v.) 捆綁
    (bind-bound-bound)

11. **wrist** [rɪst] (n.) 腰部
12. **be free to** 隨意做……；
    自由做……
13. **embarrassing** [ɪmˈbærəsɪŋ]
    (a.) 難堪的

A Match.

1 M. Gillenormand •

2 Eponine •

3 Cosette •

4 Marius •

• **a** My father says we may have to move again.

• **b** Forgive me for following you for so long.

• **c** I have a letter that Cosette asked me to give you.

• **d** Have you come to apologize to me?

B Fill in the blanks with the given words.

> overthrown   swooned   supporter
> retreated   evidence

1 Marius did not want to give _____ against Thenardier.

2 She was so overcome by his words that she _____ and fell backward.

3 Charles X was _____ by a peaceful revolution in 1830.

4 General Lamarque was a staunch _____ of democracy and Napoleon.

5 Marius lowered his torch to the barrel, and the soldiers _____.

C Choose the correct answer.

1 What was in the envelope that Marius left in Cosette's garden?

(a) A notebook of love poems
(b) A love letter
(c) A letter asking for money

2 Who built a barricade in the market district?

(a) M. Thenardier and his friends
(b) Inspector Javert and government soldiers
(c) Enjolras and his revolutionary friends

D True or False.

T F **1** Eponine refused to give Marius Cosette's address.

T F **2** Marius and Cosette met secretly in the garden of her house.

T F **3** Marius was happy when Cosette told him she would move to England.

T F **4** M. Gillenormand hoped that Marius would return to him one day.

T F **5** Marius put the gun in his pocket to shoot Jean Valjean.

The Background for the Story

To get a better understanding of *Les Misérables*, it is important to consider the historical and philosophical[1] background for the story. Eighteenth century France saw growing philosophical turmoil[2] and political[3] unrest[4]. The population was becoming increasingly aware of social injustice[5] because of the works of radical[6] writers like Voltaire, David Hume, and the like.

The ideas contained[7] in their works encouraged readers to challenge the rigid[8], religious[9] traditions[10] of society and its foundations, leading indirectly to the French revolution and the Napoleonic era which form the backdrop[11] and historical context for the events of *Les Misérables*.

1. **philosophical** [ˌfɪləˈsɑːfɪkəl] (a.) 哲學的
2. **turmoil** [ˈtɜːrmɔɪl] (n.) 混亂；騷動
3. **political** [pəˈlɪtɪkəl] (a.) 政治的
4. **unrest** [ʌnˈrest] (n.) 動盪；不安
5. **injustice** [ɪnˈdʒʌstɪs] (n.) 不公正
6. **radical** [ˈrædɪkəl] (a.) 激進的
7. **contain** [kənˈteɪn] (v.) 包含
8. **rigid** [ˈrɪdʒɪd] (a.) 死板的
9. **religious** [rɪˈlɪdʒəs] (a.) 宗教的

This work captures[12] the philosophical changes of the times as well. People wanted to move away from the cold religious dogma[13] that gave no room for sin toward a more tolerant[14] and caring approach. This movement was called the "Enlightenment[15]." This movement gave birth to the ideas that God and sin do not exist and the only truth is that humans are morally[16] free.

However, this freedom also had restrictions[17], in that it became wrong to take away anyone's freedom. So then, one might ask, how should we live our lives?

In *Les Misérables*, Hugo suggests that we begin by recognizing our responsibilities[18] toward each other, both as individuals[19] and collectively as a society. These ideas are clearly reinforced[20] in the actions of the Bishop and Jean Valjean.

10. **tradition** [trə'dɪʃən] (n.) 傳統
11. **backdrop** ['bækdrɑːp] (n.) 背景
12. **capture** ['kæptʃər] (v.) 記錄
13. **dogma** ['dɑːgmə] (n.) 教條
14. **tolerant** ['tɑːlərənt] (a.) 容忍的
15. **the Enlightenment** 啟蒙運動
16. **morally** ['mɔːrəli] (adv.) 道德上地
17. **restriction** [rɪ'strɪkʃən] (n.) 限制
18. **responsibility** [rɪ,spɑːnsə'bɪləti] (n.) 責任
19. **individual** [,ɪndɪ'vɪdʒuəl] (n.) 個人
20. **reinforce** [,riːɪn'fɔːrs] (v.) 加強

Chapter Five

🎧 40 Redemption[1]

The soldiers amassed[2] their numbers and rushed[3] the barricade. One by one, all of the rebels fell. Marius was shot in the shoulder and felt someone grab him. He thought he would be captured[4] and executed by the soldiers as he lost consciousness[5]. Enjolras swung[6] his sword defiantly[7] under a hail of[8] bullets. He was the last rebel to die.

Marius was not taken prisoner. After he was shot and passed out[9], Valjean grabbed him and pulled him into the alley behind the barricade.

There seemed to be no escape from the advancing[10] soldiers. Valjean looked all around. Then he saw the answer. There on the street was a hole covered by an iron grill[11]. Valjean

---

1. **redemption** [rɪ'dempʃən] (n.) 救贖；贖罪
2. **amass** [ə'mæs] (v.) 累積
3. **rush** [rʌʃ] (v.) 衝；闖
4. **capture** ['kæptʃər] (v.) 捕；捉
5. **consciousness** ['kɑːnʃəsnɪs] (n.) 意識
6. **swing** [swɪŋ] (v.) 揮動 (swing-swung-swung)
7. **defiantly** [dɪ'faɪəntli] (adv.) 拚命地
8. **a hail of** 一陣⋯⋯
9. **pass out** 昏倒
10. **advance** [əd'væns] (v.) 前進

lifted [12] the grill, hoisted [13]
Marius onto his shoulders,
and climbed down into the
sewers [14] of Paris.

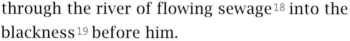

Down there it was
slippery [15] and dark.
Valjean struggled to [16] carry
Marius as he trudged [17]
through the river of flowing sewage [18] into the
blackness [19] before him.

After walking for a long time, he had to
take a rest. He stopped to bandage [20] Marius'
bleeding [21] wounds [22]. In the young man's
pocket he found a note:

*I am Marius Pontmercy. My body
should be taken to my grandfather M.
Gillenormand's house at 6 Rue des Filles-
der Calvaire in the Marais.*

11. **grill** [grɪl] (n.) 鐵架
12. **lift** [lɪft] (v.) 舉起；抬起
13. **hoist** [hɔɪst] (v.) 舉起
14. **sewer** ['suːər] (n.) 下水道
15. **slippery** ['slɪpəri] (a.) 滑的
16. **struggle to** 奮力；使勁
17. **trudge** [trʌdʒ] (v.) 跋涉

18. **sewage** ['suːɪdʒ] (n.) 污水
19. **blackness** [blæknɪs] (n.) 黑暗處
20. **bandage** ['bændɪdʒ] (v.)
    用繃帶包紮（傷口）
21. **bleeding** ['bliːdɪŋ] (a.)
    流血的
22. **wound** [wuːnd] (n.) 傷口

Valjean memorized[1] the address and continued[2] his journey[3] through the sewer toward the river. After many hours, he could see light at the end of the long tunnel[4]. But when he got there, the iron gate between the sewer and their freedom was locked. Valjean let out a cry of despair[5]. There was no way out.

Then he felt a hand on his shoulder. It was M. Thenardier. He had escaped from prison into the sewers. He showed Valjean a key to the locked iron gate he had stolen.

1. **memorize** [ˈmeməraɪz] (v.) 記住
2. **continue** [kənˈtɪnjuː] (v.) 繼續
3. **journey** [ˈdʒɜːrni] (n.) 旅程
4. **tunnel** [ˈtʌnl] (n.) 隧道
5. **despair** [dɪˈspeɪr] (n.) 絕望
6. **waste** [weɪst] (n.) 垃圾；廢物

"I see you've killed this man," said Thenardier. "I'll let you through this gate if you give me half of what you stole from his pockets."

Valjean said nothing. He reached in his pocket and gave Thenardier thirty francs. "You killed a man for this little money. What a waste[6]!" said Thenardier as he unlocked[7] the gate, and then he scurried off[8] into the sewers like a rat[9].

Valjean climbed up the riverbank[10] to the world above. There he stopped to splash[11] some water on Marius' face. But standing there was another man. It was Javert. The inspector had been chasing Thenardier after he had escaped from prison.

7. **unlock** [ʌnˈlɑːk] (v.) 開鎖
8. **scurry off** 匆忙地跑走
9. **rat** [ræt] (n.) 老鼠

10. **riverbank** [ˈrɪvərˌbæŋk] (n.) 河岸
11. **splash** [splæʃ] (v.) （水）濺

✓ *Check Up* True or False.

T F [a] Thenardier asked Valjean for money to unlock the gate.

T F [b] Javert was still following Jean Valjean after he was freed.

Ans: a. T b. F

"Please help me take this man home. He's badly injured," said Valjean. Javert looked unhappy but agreed to help him. They put Marius in a carriage[1] and told the driver the address. At the gate of M. Gillenormand's house, Valjean told Javert he could arrest him after he took the boy inside. But when Valjean returned to the waiting carriage, Inspector Javert was gone.

When M. Gillenormand saw Marius' lifeless[2] body, he cried, "He's dead, the fool! He did this to punish[3] me!"

Then a doctor examined Marius.

"He might live," the doctor said. "The wound to his body is not serious, but there are some deep cuts[4] on his head."

"Ah, my grandson!" M. Gillenormand cried with joy. "You're alive after all[5]!"

---

1. **carriage** [ˈkærɪdʒ] (n.) 馬車
2. **lifeless** [ˈlaɪfləs] (a.) 毫無生氣的
3. **punish** [ˈpʌnɪʃ] (v.) 懲罰
4. **cut** [kʌt] (n.) 傷口
5. **after all** 最終；畢竟
6. **generosity** [ˌdʒenəˈrɑːsəti] (n.) 慷慨；仁慈
7. **commit suicide** 自殺

The next morning, Javert's body was found in the river. He was an unhappy man who was unable to understand the kindness and generosity[6] of Valjean. He had committed suicide[7].

Marius spent the next three months recuperating[1].

"Grandfather," he said one day, "I still plan to marry Cosette."

"Of course, my boy," said M. Gillenormand, who had become a much kinder man since his grandson was returned to him alive. "It's all been arranged[2]. She's just waiting for you to heal[3] properly[4] as the doctor ordered. I've gotten to know[5] her and her father. I think she's a charming[6] girl."

Marius was overjoyed. Later that day, Cosette came to visit him with her father, who had a strangely nervous smile.

Their wedding[7] was set[8] to take place in February of the following year. The happy couple decided they would live with M. Gillenormand after they were married.

1. **recuperate** [rɪˈkuːpəreɪt] (v.) 恢復
2. **arrange** [əˈreɪndʒ] (v.) 安排
3. **heal** [hiːl] (v.) 治癒
4. **properly** [ˈprɑːpərli] (adv.) 適當地；正確地
5. **get to know** 認識；知曉
6. **charming** [ˈtʃɑːrmɪŋ] (a.) 迷人的；有魅力的
7. **wedding** [ˈwedɪŋ] (n.) 婚禮
8. **be set** 安排於……

For Marius, there were only two important things to do besides[9] preparing to be married. He wanted to find Thenardier. Even though he knew the man was a terrible thief[10], he desperately wanted to respect[11] his father's last wish. Secondly, he wanted to find whomever it was who saved his life on the night he was shot. He often spoke of this to Cosette and Valjean, but Valjean was always silent[12].

9. **besides** [bɪˈsaɪdz] (prep.)
   除……之外
10. **thief** [θiːf] (n.) 小偷
   （複數：thieves）

11. **respect** [rɪˈspekt] (v.)
   尊敬；尊重
12. **silent** [ˈsaɪlənt] (a.) 沉默的

The night of the wedding was wonderful.
The only thing that made Cosette unhappy
was that Valjean had said he felt ill and had
gone home before the feast[1].

Valjean was at home crying.
He remembered the little girl he had rescued[2]
from the Thenardiers ten years earlier. He felt
very sad that he was no longer[3] the most
important man in her life. And he remembered
that he was Jean Valjean, a criminal who had
spent nineteen years in prison and who had
stolen the silverware from the kind bishop's
house.

Not even Cosette knew the truth about him. If she and Marius knew, he would lose their love and respect. But if he didn't tell the truth, he felt he would lose his own soul.

The next day, Valjean went to talk to Marius. He told the young man everything about his past[4] life.

"You must promise not to tell her," said Valjean.

"I won't tell her," said Marius, "but you shouldn't spend very much time around her any more."

"Oh, but you must let me see her sometimes," begged Valjean. "Without her, I'd have nothing to live for."

"You may visit her for a short time in the evenings," said Marius.

1. **feast** [fiːst] (n.) 宴席
2. **rescue** [ˈreskjuː] (v.) 拯救
3. **no longer** 不再
4. **past** [pæst] (a.) 過去的

Without her, I'd have nothing to live for.
沒有她，我就沒有活著的理由了。

without：沒有（物或人）

e.g. **Without air, we could not live.**
沒有空氣，我們就活不了。

45

In the evenings, Valjean would come to visit
Cosette in a small room with two chairs and a
fire. She begged him to come and live with
them, but he always declined[1]. He would not
even let her call him "father" any more. "You
have a husband now. You don't need a father."

But as she now called him "Monseiur Jean", he gradually[2] became a different person to her. She began to accept his visits less and less. After some time, they stopped visiting altogether.

Marius felt it was good to get Valjean out of Cosette's life. In his private[3] research[4] on Valjean, he knew that Valjean's fortune[5] came from a wealthy Mayor Madeline, who had disappeared. After learning this fact, he would not let Cosette use any of the money Valjean had given her.

Then one evening, a servant brought Marius a letter and said the writer was waiting in the hall[6]. The letter smelled of cheap tobacco and had some familiar handwriting. When he met the visitor, he was shocked[7] to find M. Thenardier. The terrible man was there to ask for money.

1. **decline** [dɪˈklaɪn] (v.) 婉拒
2. **gradually** [ˈgrædʒuəli] (adv.) 逐漸地
3. **private** [ˈpraɪvɪt] (a.) 私人的
4. **research** [rɪˈsɜːrtʃ] (n.) 調查
5. **fortune** [ˈfɔːrtʃən] (n.) 財富
6. **hall** [hɔːl] (n.) 大廳
7. **shocked** [ʃɑːkt] (a.) 震驚的

46

"I have some interesting information to tell you about your wife's father," said M. Thenardier.

"I already know about him," said Marius.

"But the man who you think is your wife's guardian is actually a murderer[1] and a thief named[2] Jean Valjean."

"I know," said Marius, "I'm aware that[3] he robbed[4] a wealthy factory owner[5] named Mayor Madeline and that he executed Inspector Javert."

"That is incorrect[6]," said Thenardier. "He didn't rob Mayor Madeline. He was Mayor Madeline! And he didn't kill Inspector Javert. Javert killed himself."

Thenardier showed Marius a newspaper clipping[7] he had about the inspector's suicide. "But he did kill a young man whose body I saw him carrying through the sewer. I even have a piece of the young man's coat as proof[8]."

---

1. **murderer** ['mɜːrdərər] (n.) 殺人犯
2. **named** [neɪmd] 叫做……
3. **be aware that** 知曉……
4. **rob** [rɑːb] (v.) 搶奪 (rob-robbed-robbed)
5. **owner** ['oʊnər] (n.) 老闆
6. **incorrect** [ˌɪnkə'rekt] (a.) 錯誤的
7. **clipping** ['klɪpɪŋ] (n.) 剪報
8. **proof** [pruːf] (n.) 證據
9. **bloody** ['blʌdi] (a.) 染血的
10. **scrap** [skræp] (n.) 碎片

Then Thenardier showed Marius the bloody[9] scrap[10] coat. Marius recognized it as his own.

"That young man was me!" cried Marius.

He suddenly realized that Valjean was the man who had saved his life.

🎧 47

Marius gave Thenardier enough money to take his remaining[1] daughter, Azelma, to America and start a new life. Then he ran to Cosette and told her everything.

1. **remaining** [rɪˈmeɪnɪŋ] (a.)
   剩下的
2. **slump** [slʌmp] (v.) 沉重地坐下
3. **tear** [tɪr] (n.) 眼淚

4. **guilt** [gɪlt] (n.) 愧疚
5. **shame** [ʃeɪm] (n.) 羞愧
6. **ashamed** [əˈʃeɪmd] (a.)
   難為情的；羞愧的

"Your father was the man who saved me! We must go to him at once!"

When they knocked at Jean Valjean's door, they heard a weak voice say, "Come in."

"Father," cried Cosette, who ran to the old man who slumped[2] in a chair.

"So you've decided to forgive me," said Valjean.

Marius cried tears[3] of guilt[4] and shame[5], "Oh, I'm so ashamed[6]. Valjean, why didn't you tell me that I owed you my life[7]?"

"I didn't want you to be obliged to[8] a worthless[9] criminal!" said Valjean.

"You're going to come and live with us," said Marius.

"This time you can't refuse," said Cosette. But when she took his hands in hers, they were very cold. "Oh, are you ill, Father?"

7. owe *A B*
欠 A（人）B（物）
8. be obliged to 對……感激

9. worthless [ˈwɜːrθləs] (a.)
不值得的；無價值的

"No, not ill," said Valjean. "I'm dying. But to die is nothing. Not to live is terrible."

Valjean's breathing[1] became difficult. He pointed to a nearby table.

"Cosette, I want you to have those silver candlesticks. The person who gave them to me is watching us now. I hope he is pleased[2]. Now, Cosette, the time has come for me to tell you about your mother. Her name was Fantine. You mustn't forget it. She loved you very much and suffered[3] greatly. Her great sorrow[4] was as much as your great happiness is now. God balances[5] things that way. I will leave you now, but remember to always love each other. Love is the only thing that matters[6] in life."

Cosette and Marius knelt beside Valjean, weeping as the final breath[7] escaped from his lips[8]. In the light of the two candlesticks, they could see on his face a peaceful smile.

1. **breathing** ['briːðɪŋ] (n.) 呼吸
2. **pleased** [pliːzd] (a.) 愉悅的
3. **suffer** ['sʌfər] (v.) 受苦
4. **sorrow** ['sɑːroʊ] (n.) 悲傷
5. **balance** ['bæləns] (v.) 平衡
6. **matter** ['mætər] (v.) 要緊;有關係
7. **breath** [breθ] (n.) 呼吸
8. **lip** [lɪp] (n.) 嘴唇

✅ *Check Up* Fill in the blanks with proper words.

Valjean's last words to Marius and Cosette were that they should always _____ _____ _____.

Ans: love each other

One Point Lesson

> I will leave you now, but **remember to** always love each other.
> 我現在就要離開妳了，但是記得永遠要珍愛彼此。

---

remember + to V：記得要去做某個動作

remember + Ving：記得做過某個動作

e.g. I **remember meeting** him at the park.
我記得在公園見過他。

121

A Match.

1 Jean Valjean •

• **a** You may visit her for a short time in the evenings.

2 M. Thenardier •

• **b** She's just waiting for you to heal properly as the doctor ordered.

3 Marius •

• **c** I have some interesting information about your wife's father.

4 M. Gillenormand •

• **d** To die is nothing. Not to live is terrible.

B True or False.

T F **1** Marius was unable to heal from his wounds at the barricade.

T F **2** M. Gillenormand thought Cosette was a charming girl.

T F **3** Jean Valjean told Cosette the truth about his past as a criminal.

T F **4** After learning about Valjean's past, Marius thought it was good to get Valjean out of Cosette's life.

T F **5** Valjean died with a sad frown on his face.

C Choose the correct answer.

❶ Why didn't Marius allow Cosette to spend the money Valjean had given her?

(a) Because he wanted to earn their own money.

(b) Because he felt they didn't need the money.

(c) Because he thought the money had been stolen from Mayor Madeline.

❷ Why didn't Valjean tell Marius that he had saved his life?

(a) Because he was waiting for the right time to tell him.

(b) Because he didn't want Marius to feel obligated to a worthless criminal.

(c) Because Marius hated Valjean and wanted him to die.

D Fill in the blanks with the given words.

bandage	recuperate	execute	decline

❶ Jean Valjean stopped to _____ Marius' bleeding wounds.

❷ Marius spent the next three months _____.

❸ She begged Valjean to come and live with them, but he always _____.

❹ Marius thought that Valjean had _____ Javert.

1 Basic Grammar

要增強英文閱讀理解能力，應練習找出英文的主結構。
要擁有良好的英語閱讀能力，首先要理解英文的段落結構。

「英文的閱讀理解從『分解文章』開始。」

　　英文的文章是以「有意義的詞組」（指帶有意義的語句）所構成的。下面用（／）符號來區別各個意義語塊，請試著掌握其中的意義。

He knew / that she told a lie / at the party.

他知道　　　　她說了謊　　　　在舞會上
⇨ 他知道她在舞會上說謊的事。

As she was walking / in the garden, / she smelled /

當她行走　　　　　　在花園　　　　她聞到味道

something wet.

某樣東西濕濕的
⇨ 她走在花園時聞到潮溼的味道。

He knew / that she told a lie / at the party.

他知道　／她說了一個謊　　／在那個派對上。

一篇文章，要分成幾個有意義的詞組？
可放入（／）符號來區隔有意義詞組的地方，一般是在（1）「主詞＋動詞」之後；（2）and 和 but 等連接詞之前；（3）that、who 等關係代名詞之前；（4）副詞子句的前後。初學者可能在一篇文章中畫很多（／）符號，但隨著閱讀實力的提升，（／）會減少。時間一久，在不太複雜的文章中即使不畫（／）符號，也能一眼就理解整句的意義。

使用（／）符號來閱讀理解英語篇章
1. 能熟悉英文的句型和構造。
2. 可加速閱讀速度。

該方法對於需要邊聽理解的英文聽力也有很好的效果。
從現在開始，早日丟棄過去理解文章的習慣吧！

以直接閱讀理解的方式，重新閱讀《悲慘世界》

　　從原文中摘錄一小段。以具有意義的詞組將文章做斷句區分，重新閱讀並做理解練習。

One cold evening in October of 1815, / a man with a long beard
1815 年十月裡的一個寒冷傍晚，　　　　　／一個留著長鬍子、穿著髒衣服的男人

and dirty clothes / walked into the French town of Digne. //
　　　　　　　　　／走進了法國笛涅這個小鎮。//

The man was in his forties / and very strong. //
這個人大約四十多歲　　　　／長得很壯。//

He carried a bag and a walking staff. //

他揹了一個背包，拄了根拐杖。//

The man entered an inn / and said to the innkeeper, //

這個人走進一家客棧 　　 / 向客棧老闆說：//

"I've been traveling / for a long time, / and I'm very tired. //

「我走了 　　　　 / 好長一段時間， / 很累。//

I need a meal and a place to sleep. // I have money to pay you." //

我需要吃頓飯，找個地方睡。　　　 // 我有錢可以付你。」//

The innkeeper looked closely / at the strange man. //

客棧老闆湊近瞧了瞧 　　　 / 這個陌生人。//

"I know / who you are. // You are Jean Valjean. //

「我知道 / 你是誰。　 // 你是尚萬強。//

You've just been released / from prison. //

你剛被放出來 　　　　 / 從監獄裡。//

I don't serve people / like you! // Get out of here / immediately!" //

我不接待 　　　 / 像你這樣的人！// 出去 　　 / 馬上！//

Jean Valjean left peacefully. //

尚萬強平靜地離開。//

Outside it was dark, cold, and windy. //

外面一片漆黑，很冷，還刮著風。//

He was desperate / for a place to rest. //

他非常想 　　　 / 找到一個休息的地方。//

He lay down / on a stone bench / in front of a church /

他躺在 　　 / 石頭長椅上 　　　 / 教堂前的 /

and tried to sleep. //

想入睡。//

But a woman came out and asked, /

但是一個婦人走出來問他：/

"How can you sleep outside / on that stone bench?" //

「你怎麼有辦法睡在外面　　/ 的石椅上？」//

"I've been sleeping / on a wooden one in prison /

「我已經睡　　　　/ 在監獄的木板椅上 /

for nineteen years. // What's the difference?" //

十九年了。　　　　// 這兩者有什麼差別？」//

The woman pointed to a small house / next to the church. //

那個婦人指著一間小屋　　　　　　/ 教堂旁。//

"You could stay there," / she said. //

「你可以待在那裡。」　/ 她說。//

The Bishop of Digne was a gentle, old man /

笛涅鎮的主教是個和善的老人 /

who lived with his sister and a servant. //

他和妹妹及僕人住在一起。//

He helped anyone / who was in need, /

他幫助所有　　　/ 需要被幫助的人，/

and he never locked his doors. //

而且他從來不鎖門。//

Guide to Listening Comprehension

 When listening to the story, use some of the techniques shown below. If you take time to study some phonetic characteristics of English, listening will be easier.

Get in the flow of English.

English creates a rhythm formed by combinations of strong and weak stress intonations. Each word has its particular stress that combines with other words to form the overall pattern of stress or rhythm in a particular sentence.

When you are speaking and listening to English, it is essential to get in the flow of the rhythm of English. It takes a lot of practice to get used to such a rhythm. So, you need to start by identifying the stressed syllable in a word.

Listen for the strongly stressed words and phrases.

In English, key words and phrases that are essential to the meaning of a sentence are stressed louder. Therefore, pay attention to the words stressed with a higher pitch. When listening to an English recording for the first time, what matters most is to listen for a general understanding of what you hear. Do not try to hear every single word. Most of the unstressed words are articles or auxiliary verbs, which don't play an important role in the general context. At this level, you can ignore them.

Pay attention to liaisons.

In reading English, words are written with a space between them. There isn't such an obvious guide when it comes to listening to English. In oral English, there are many cases when the sounds of words are linked with adjacent words.

For instance, let's think about the phrase "take off," which can be used in "take off your clothes." "Take off your clothes" doesn't sound like [teɪk ɔːf] with each of the words completely and clearly separated from the others. Instead, it sounds as if almost all the words in context are slurred together, [ˈteɪkɔːf], for a more natural sound.

Shadow the voice of the native speaker.

Finally, you need to mimic the voice of the native speaker. Once you are sure you know how to pronounce all the words in a sentence, try to repeat them like an echo. Listen to the book again, but this time you should try a fun exercise while listening to the English.

This exercise is called "shadowing." The word "shadow" means a dark shade that is formed on a surface. When used as a verb, the word refers to the action of following someone or something like a shadow. In this exercise, pretend you are a parrot and try to shadow the voice of the native speaker.

Try to mimic the reader's voice by speaking at the same speed, with the same strong and weak stresses on words, and pausing or stopping at the same points.

Experts have already proven this technique to be effective. If you practice this shadowing exercise, your English speaking and listening skills will improve by leaps and bounds. While shadowing the native speaker, don't forget to pay attention to the meaning of each phrase and sentence.

Listen to what you want to shadow many times. Start out by just trying to shadow a few words or a sentence.

 Mimic the CD out loud. You can shadow everything the speaker says as if you are singing a round, or you also can speak simultaneously with the recorded voice of the native speaker.

 As you practice more, try to shadow more. For instance, shadow a whole sentence or paragraph instead of just a few words.

Listening Guide

CHAPTER ONE : page 14–15 🎧49

One cold evening in October of (❶), a man with a long beard and dirty clothes (❷) (　) the French town of Digne. The man was in his forties and very strong. He carried a bag and a walking staff.

The man entered an inn and (❸) (　) the innkeeper, "I've been traveling for a long time, and I'm very tired. I need a meal and a place to sleep. I have money to pay you."

The innkeeper looked closely at the (❹) (　). "I know who you are. You are Jean Valjean. You've just been released from prison. I don't serve people like you! (❺) (　) (　) here immediately!"

Jean Valjean left peacefully. Outside it was dark, cold, and windy. He was desperate for a place to rest. He lay down on a stone bench (❻) (　) (　) a church and tried to sleep. But a woman came out and asked, "How can you sleep outside on that stone bench?"

"I've been sleeping on a wooden one in prison for nineteen years. What's the difference?"

以下為《悲慘世界》各章節的前半部。一開始若能聽清楚發音，之後就沒有聽力的負擔。先聽過摘錄的章節，之後再反覆聆聽括弧內單字的發音，並仔細閱讀各種發音的說明。以下都是以英語的典型發音為基礎所做的簡易說明，即使這裡未提到的發音，也可以配合音檔反覆聆聽，如此一來聽力必能更上層樓。

❶ **1815**：年份 1815 發音為 eighteen-fifteen，亦即年份的前兩碼和後兩碼分開讀，前兩碼變成 18（eighteen），後兩碼變成 15（fifteen）。要留意 eighteen 和 eighty 的發音差別，eighteen 發音為 [ˌeɪˈtiːn]，其重音在第二音節，「teen」發長音 [iː]；eighty 發音為 [ˈeɪti]，其重音在第一音節，「ty」發短音 [i]。

❷ **walked into**：動詞 walk 的字尾是無聲子音 [k]，其過去式 walked 要讀成 [wɔːkt]，過去式字尾「-ed」發音成 [t]。又 walked 後面的 into 以母音發音開頭 [ˈɪntuː]，所以在口語中的連音變成 [ˈwɔːkˈtɪntuː]。

❸ **said to**：say 的過去式 said，發音為 [sed]，因其字尾是有聲子音 [d]，而 said 後面的 to 為子音發音，為求講話發音的流暢，在口語連音中往往不發出 [d] 的音，而是做一個快速的頓音滑過去。

❹ **strange man**：strange 音標 [streɪndʒ]，但在實際發音中，s- 後面的字母是無聲子音（包括 [t]、[p]、[k]）時，要讀成有聲子音。因此，strange 讀起來會變成 [sdreɪndʒ]。

❺ **Get out of**：這個片語連音讀起來變成 [geˈtaʊtəːv]。

❻ **in front of**：這個片語連音讀起來變成 [ɪnˈfrʌntəːv]。

The woman pointed to a small house (❶) (   ) the church. "You could stay there," she said.

The Bishop of Digne was a gentle, old man who lived with his sister and a servant. He helped anyone who was (❷) (   ), and he never locked his doors.

That evening, he was sitting by the fire when his sister said, "Brother, people are saying there's a terrible man in town. The police (❸) (   ) everyone to lock their doors and windows."

But the bishop only smiled. Suddenly there was a loud knock at the door.

"Come in," said the bishop.

The bishop's sister and servant trembled when Jean Valjean walked into their house, but the bishop was calm.

"I am Jean Valjean," said the stranger. "I've (❹) (   ) released from prison after nineteen years. I've been walking for four days, and I (❺) need a place to rest. Can you help me?"

The bishop told his servant to set (❻) place at the table for Valjean. "Sit down, and warm yourself, Monsieur Valjean," said the bishop. "Dinner will be ready soon."

❶ **next to**：next 的發音為 [nɛkst]，因為其字尾的音 [t]，與後面的字 to 的字首音相同，所以連音起來變成只發一個 [t] 的音。

❷ **in need**：這一條的發音變化原則同上述的 next to。in 的字尾 [n]，音同 need 的字首發音，故合而只發一個 [n] 的音。

❸ **have told**：told 是 tell 的過去分詞，tell（告訴）是及物動詞，後面要接受詞。其常接受詞 you、him、her，told 的字尾 [d] 會和這些受詞連音讀起來。

❹ **just been**：just 的 t 為無聲子音，後面接 been 發音時，[t] 省略不發音，念起來為 jusbeen。

❺ **desperately**：desperately 的音標是 ['dɛspərɪtli]。當音標遇到有 [tl]、[tn] 連在一起發音時，t 的音都會輕輕滑過。

❻ **another**：發音為 [ə'nʌðər]，a 發短母音 [ə]，所以重音在後。

4

Listening
Comprehension

🎧 ⓐ **Listen to the CD. Write down the sentences and names.**

❶ _____(   )

❷ _____(   )

❸ _____(   )

❹ _____(   )

❺ _____(   )

🎧 ⓑ **Listen to the CD and choose the correct answer.**

❶ _____ ?

    (a) Thanks for catching this criminal. Put him in prison.

    (b) He did not steal the silverware. I gave it to him freely.

    (c) I think he took some of my money, too.

❷ _____ ?

    (a) Because they wanted to support Napoleon.

    (b) Because they wanted to pay less taxes.

    (c) Because King Louis-Phillipe failed to understand the needs of the poor.

🎧 53 **C** Listen to the CD and fill in the blanks.

1 The bishop's sister and servant _____ when Valjean walked into their house, but the bishop was _____.

2 Javert and the mayor _____, but Fantine was finally _____.

3 _____, it was the same room that Valjean and Cosette had lived in three years _____.

4 She found an _____ that contained a small notebook filled with love _____.

5 Cosette and Marius _____ beside Valjean, _____ as the final breath escaped from his lips.

🎧 54 **D** Listen to the CD. True or False.

T F ①

T F ②

T F ③

T F ④

T F ⑤

維克多·雨果（Victor Hugo, 1802–1885）

　　維克多·雨果是法國著名詩人、小說家及劇作家。雨果在家中排行老三，父親是拿破崙軍隊裡的高階長官，母親是極端的天主教保皇主義者。雨果對文學很有興趣，但父親希望他從軍。

　　1822 年，雨果發表第一部詩集《頌詩與雜詠集》（*Odes et Poésies Diverses*），之後 20 年餘，出版了許多詩集、小說與劇作。他的女兒在 1843 年去世，而在之後十年裡一直潛心於政治。

　　1851 年拿破崙三世掌權，制訂了反國會制的憲法，雨果遂批他為法國的叛國賊。離開法國流亡在外的 19 年裡，雨果專心寫作，此時期也廣出佳作。小說《悲慘世界》（*Les Misérables,* 1862）與《鐘樓怪人》（*Notre-Dame de Paris,* 1831）被認為是雨果最傑出的作品。

　　1885 年 5 月 22 日雨果於巴黎辭世，享壽 83 歲。他得到國葬的禮遇，受到兩百萬巴黎人悼念，並葬於先賢祠（Pantheon）。

　　《悲慘世界》（*Les Misérables*）被公認為 19 世紀最偉大的小說，法文書名也被英譯成 *The Miserable Ones*（悲慘的人們）、*The Poor Ones*（可憐的人們）或 *The Wretched Poor*（可憐的貧窮人），全書五部曲共十冊。

　　本書隱含雨果對社會與宗教生活的想法，他充滿熱情地描述理想社會的建立，也為低階層的人民奮筆疾書。

　　本書主要的劇情環繞著一名叫做尚萬強的前科犯。尚萬強是個窮苦的男子，曾為了飢餓的家人偷了條麵包，並因此入獄。出獄後，他懷著報復社會的心盜竊主教的銀器，卻受到主教的原諒與釋放。

最終，尚萬強改過自新並展開新生活，成為富有的工廠老闆，並被選為當地的鎮長。

然而某一天，一位無辜的男人被指控為尚萬強，遭到逮捕，隔天將面臨審問。為了拯救這個無辜的人，真正的前科犯尚萬強決定參與審問，並揭露他的真實身分。尚萬強立刻就被逮捕入牢，但很快便逃獄了。

之後他遇見他工廠的女工芳婷，及其女兒柯賽特，並讓柯賽特逃離成為妓女的命運，三人和樂同住。然而，警探賈維卻不停追捕著尚萬強……

人物介紹

p. 12–13

Jean Valjean 尚萬強

我在獄中度過了十九年，但現在我出來了，我想要改變我的人生，成為一個好人。我努力幫助窮人，並照顧我親愛的柯賽特。

Cosette 柯賽特

我在康乃迪家的客棧裡長大，一直缺乏關愛，但尚萬強把我救出來了。我們一起過著快樂的生活，只是我們不停搬家，彷彿我們在躲著什麼似的。

Inspector Javert 警探賈維

我是一名警探，我已經追捕尚萬強好幾年了。不知為什麼，他好像總是可以逃過我的追捕，但我不會放棄的。如果有什麼事是我必須做的，那就是找到他。

Marius 馬里歐

雖然我再也無法和我外公和平共處，但無所謂，因為我愛柯賽特，我想和她結婚。只是她和她的父親一直在搬家，要找到她很不容易。

Thenardier 康乃迪

自從尚萬強把柯賽特帶走後，我們家就過得很困苦。我必須做很多事來為家人籌錢，包括偷竊。

[第一章] 兩個絕望的靈魂

p. 14—15 1815 年十月裡的一個寒冷傍晚，一個留著長鬍子、穿著髒衣服的男人，走進了法國笛涅這個小鎮。這個人大約四十多歲，長得很壯。他揹了一個背包，拄了根拐杖。

這個人走進一家客棧，向客棧老闆說：「我走了好長一段時間，很累。我需要吃頓飯，找個地方睡。我有錢可以付你。」

客棧老闆湊近瞧了瞧這個陌生人：「我知道你是誰，你是尚萬強，剛從監獄裡被放出來。我才不接待像你這樣的人！馬上出去！」

尚萬強平靜地離開了。外面一片漆黑，很冷，還刮著風。他非常想找到一個休息的地方。他躺在教堂前的石頭長椅上想入睡，但是一個婦人走過來問他：「你怎麼有辦法睡在外面的石椅上呢？」

「我已經在監獄的木板椅上睡了十九年了。這兩者有什麼差別呢？」

p. 16-17 那個婦人指著教堂旁的小屋，對他說：「你可以待在那裡。」

笛涅鎮的主教是個和善的老人，他和妹妹及僕人住在一起。他幫助所有需要幫助的人，而且從來不鎖門。

那天傍晚，主教坐在爐火旁，他的妹妹對他說：「哥哥，大家都說鎮上來了一個可怕的人，警察要大家鎖好門窗。」

主教聽了只是微笑不語。這時突然傳來很大的敲門聲。

「請進。」主教說。

當尚萬強走進他們的屋子裡時，主教的妹妹和僕人嚇得打哆嗦，但主教卻很鎮定。

陌生人說：「我是尚萬強，我被關了十九年，剛從監獄裡被放出來。我已經走了四天的路了，我非常需要一個休息的地方。你能幫幫我嗎？」

主教於是叫僕人拿張椅子，放在餐桌前給尚萬強坐下。主教說：「請坐，讓你自己暖和些，尚萬強先生，晚餐很快就準備好了。」

p. 18-19 吃過一頓大餐後，尚萬強放鬆了些，環顧了這個小房子。主教的房子並不豪華，但他看到桌上有一套貴重的銀刀、銀叉和燭台。接著，他還注意到主教的僕人把那套銀器收進櫥櫃。

主教遞給尚萬強一個燭台，說道：「拿著，這可以照路，跟我去客房吧。」

當他們到房間後，主教對他說：「晚安，別忘了明天離開之前，來喝碗我們的新鮮牛奶。」

尚萬強累到沒換衣服就睡著了。儘管筋疲力盡，他卻只睡幾個小時就醒了。因為睡不著，他開始回想自己的過去。生活一直對他很不公平，他仍為此感到忿忿不平。

1795 年，他失去了筏木工作。當時，他得幫忙撫養守寡的妹妹和她的七個小孩。為了撫養他們，他偷了幾條麵包卻銀鐺入獄，也因此失去了生命中最美好的歲月。

p. 20–21 尚萬強想對這個世界報仇！然後他想到主教那套值錢的銀器，心中突然浮現了一個計畫。

尚萬強離開床舖，光著腳，躡手躡腳地走在屋子裡。他手上拿著一根一端尖銳的短鐵條，走進主教的房間裡，將鐵條高舉在那個沉睡的人頭上，但主教沉睡的臉看起來如此祥和仁慈，讓他無法下手殺害他。於是，他把那些值錢的銀刀和銀叉塞進他的背包裡，用爬的穿過後花園逃走了。

隔天早上，主教難過地看著花園裡那些在尚萬強逃走時被踩爛的花朵。

僕人大叫：「主教，您知道您那些貴重的銀器被偷了嗎？一定是昨晚在這裡過夜的那個人拿走的！」

主教說：「是，我知道，但我想那是我自己的錯，我霸佔那些昂貴的銀器太久了。」

那天早上稍晚時，四個警察和尚萬強回到主教的房子。警察小隊長說：「主教，我們抓到這個帶著一些貴重銀器的犯人。這些東西是您的嗎？」

主教對尚萬強微笑說：「親愛的朋友，你忘記帶走這些銀燭台了，它們至少可以讓你換得兩百法郎啊！」

p. 22-23 尚萬強和那些警察都不可置信地張大了眼睛。「先生，您是說，是您把銀器給這個人的？」警官問。

「是的，一點也沒錯。你得放他走。」

隨後，那些警察就離開了。主教走近尚萬強並說道：「現在，你必須用這些錢讓你自己成為一個誠實的人。我從惡魔那裡把你的靈魂買來，並且將它交給了上帝。」

尚萬強在鄉間徘徊著，感到十分困惑。當這世界對他不公平，他為此感到憤怒時，他慢慢可以理解和接受發生的所有一切。然而，有那麼大的恩惠賜予他時，他反而不知道該怎麼辦才好了。

當他越過一大片原野時，尚萬強碰到了一個十歲大的男孩，那男孩邊走邊吹口哨，還開心地將一個銀幣丟到空中再接住。尚萬強伸出他的手，接住了那男孩的硬幣。

「先生，請把我的銅板還給我。我只是個掃煙囪的工人，那是我所有的錢了。」

「走開。」尚萬強說。

「先生……拜託！」男孩哭著說。

尚萬強舉起拐杖要打男孩，男孩嚇得跑掉了。等到男孩遠離他的視線後，他看看自己手裡的銅板，不敢相信自己剛剛做了什麼。他要叫那個男孩回來，但是他已經不見了。他筋疲力竭地坐在石頭上，十九年來第一次，他哭了。

p. 24-25 1818 年，在靠近巴黎一個叫做蒙佛梅的小村莊裡，有兩個小女孩正在盪鞦韆。那是一個美好的春日傍晚。她們的母親是名滿頭紅髮、長相平庸的女子。她坐在附近，從他們住的客棧前面看著她們。

突然有個少婦走向她，說道：「夫人，妳的女兒們真漂亮。」

這位少婦臂彎裡抱著一個沉睡的小孩。她看起來既可憐又悲傷。

　　女孩們的母親說：「謝謝妳，坐下來休息一下，妳看起來很累。」

　　那位少婦坐下，並且介紹了自己。她的名字叫芳婷。

　　有兩個女兒的婦人說：「我是康乃迪太太，我和丈夫一起經營這家客棧。」

　　芳婷告訴婦人，自己之前在巴黎工作，但是她丈夫過世了，她也失去了工作。不過她其實在說謊，事實上，她是和一個年輕人有了孩子卻被始亂終棄。在那個年代，一個帶著孩子的未婚媽媽是很辛苦的。

　　隨後，芳婷的小女兒醒了過來。她的眼睛就像母親一樣，又大又藍。小女孩咯咯地笑著，然後從她母親的膝上跳下來，跑去和鞦韆上的兩個女孩玩了起來。

p. 26–27「妳女兒叫什麼名字？」康乃迪太太問。

　　「她叫柯賽特，快三歲了。」

　　這兩個女人看著她們的孩子一起玩耍，康乃迪太太笑著說：「看看她們這麼快就玩在一起了，她們應該當姊妹的。」

　　這些話讓芳婷做出了奇怪的舉動，她突然緊握康乃迪太太的手，問道：「妳有沒有可能幫我照顧她？我必須找到一份工作，但是這對一個帶著小孩、又沒有丈夫的女人來說，幾乎是不可能的。我一找到工作就會來接她的。我有足夠的錢，可以每個月付妳六法郎！」

　　康乃迪太太沒有回答，她不知道該說什麼，這時她的丈夫站在她背後說道：「如果妳能預付六個月的錢，我們可以以一個月七法郎的代價來照顧她。」

芳婷從她的錢包裡拿出錢來。

隔天早上，芳婷向她的女兒說再見，親吻著她，哭得好像她的心都碎了一樣。

康乃迪先生對太太說：「我們需要這筆錢，現在我可以償還債務，不必坐牢了。妳騙得不錯喔！」

「我一開始並不打算這麼做。」他太太回答。

p. 28–29 一個月後，康乃迪先生需要更多的錢，所以他把柯賽特的衣服賣了，換得六十法郎。他們讓那小女孩穿得破破爛爛的，而且叫她和小狗小貓們一起在桌子底下吃剩菜剩飯。

就在此時，芳婷開始在遠處一個城裡的工廠工作，她每個月都會寄信和錢給女兒。康乃迪夫婦開始要求更多的錢，而芳婷也十分樂意地支付。他們告訴芳婷，他們待她很好。但事實上，他們對自己的女兒艾潘妮和亞薩瑪很好，但他們對待柯賽特卻像奴隸一樣。

芳婷在工廠裡小心地保守她有女兒的秘密。但那裡的婦人最後還是發現她是個未婚媽媽，並且告訴了所有人。芳婷被解僱了，而且到處都找不到其他的工作。

為了省下一點錢寄給柯賽特，那年冬天芳婷在她小小的房間裡，完全不點柴火，勉強度日。她靠著縫衣服賺了點錢，但還不夠，所以她去一家假髮店賣了自己的頭髮，換得十法郎。

這時，她又收到一封康乃迪夫婦寄來的信，信上說柯賽特病得很嚴重，需要四十法郎買藥。這個消息讓芳婷非常著急，於是她賣掉了她的兩顆門牙。

在她賣掉頭髮和門牙之後，芳婷已經沒有什麼方法可以賺錢了。康乃迪夫婦仍然持續地要錢，所以芳婷開始賣她唯一剩下的東西——她的身體。

[第二章] 守護者

p. 32–33 一個寒冷的冬夜裡，一名沒有牙齒、看起來很貧窮的婦人，因為在街上攻擊一名男性而被逮捕。在警察局裡，警探賈維決定把那名婦人關進監獄六個月。

那個婦人哭喊著：「請不要把我送進牢裡。如果我沒償還我所欠的錢，我的女兒就會沒有家，要流落街頭了。」

警探賈維並不理會她，還叫手下把她帶走。這時，突然有一個聲音說道：「請等一下。當時街上所發生的事我都看到了，是那個男人的錯，不是這個女人的錯。」

警探賈維抬頭看著馬德琳鎮長。他是這個鎮上地位最高的人。

在他成為本鎮的鎮長之前，馬德琳先生是在 1815 年的一個冬夜裡，突然來到這個小鎮的。當時他身無分文，卻知道一種可以用低成本製造玻璃的新方法。幾個月內，他的新玻璃工廠讓他變成有錢人，而他又用這些錢蓋了兩座新工廠，並為鎮上帶來上百個工作機會。

他自己過著簡樸的生活，並把大部分的錢都用來蓋醫院和學校。在 1820 年時，鎮民們選他當鎮長。

p. 34–35 但是鎮上有個人並不喜歡馬德琳鎮長。警探賈維一直懷疑這個曾經陌生的人，他覺得他以前有看過鎮長這張臉，好像是早期的一個危險罪犯。

現在，馬德琳鎮長就在警探賈維的警局裡，他想要拯救芳婷免於牢獄之災。但是當芳婷看到鎮長時，她卻朝他吐口水：「就是你的工廠讓我丟掉工作的。現在我成為了一個壞女人，永遠也要不回我的女兒了。」

賈維和鎮長力爭著，最後芳婷被釋放了。隨後，馬德琳鎮長對芳婷說：「我不是故意要造成妳的麻煩，我會幫助妳，幫妳償還債務，並且幫妳把女兒帶回來。在上帝的眼裡，妳絕對不是一個壞女人。」

鎮長所給予的寬厚仁慈，讓芳婷哭了，她跪下來親吻他的手。

鎮長寄給康乃迪夫婦三百法郎，並叫他們馬上把柯賽特送到他身邊。但是康乃迪先生回信要求五百法郎，馬德琳鎮長也把錢寄過去了，但康乃迪夫婦並沒有把柯賽特送回來。

p. 36–37 儘管芳婷就快重拾幸福，但是長年的悲慘與窮困，讓她變得非常虛弱。她病得很重，無法從床上起身。每當馬德琳鎮長來探望她時，她總是問：「我什麼時候可以見到柯賽特？」

「就快了。」他說。聽到這裡，她總是開心地微笑。

有一天早上，馬德琳鎮長正準備親自到康乃迪夫婦所住的鎮上接回柯賽特時，賈維警探突然走進他的辦公室。

「我要為長久以來一直懷疑您而道歉。」警探說。

「你在說什麼？」馬德琳鎮長問道。

「多年來，我一直懷疑你就是那個逃亡的罪犯尚萬強。但是現在另一個鎮的警方已經抓到真正的尚萬強了。那個人說他的名字叫強曼森，但有幾位目擊證人說他就是尚萬強，他明天就要面對審判了，而且要在監獄裡度過終身。我對自己一直懷疑您而感到抱歉。」

p. 38–39 警探離開後，馬德琳鎮長取消了隔天去拜訪康乃迪夫婦的行程。當晚，他躺在床上輾轉難眠，馬德琳市長事實上就是尚萬強，他不能讓那個叫做強曼森的人為自己的罪行在牢裡度過餘生。他必須參加那個人的審判，承認一切的罪行。他會失去他努力的一切，但他別無選擇。真相才是最重要的。

隔天早上，馬德琳鎮長到了舉行審判的小鎮上。當他抵達時，他看到那個強曼森只是個高大的男孩，不夠聰明，所以無法為自己辯護。正當法官就要宣判強曼森就是尚萬強時，馬德琳鎮長站了起來，說：「這個人不是尚萬強，我才是。」

整個法庭都可以聽到眾人倒抽一口氣的聲音。一開始，沒有人相信他的話，於是他告訴大家一些只有尚萬強才會知道的事情。

「現在我必須走了，」馬德琳鎮長說：「我有一些事情要辦。等我的事情都辦妥後，我決對不會逃跑的。」

他們讓他離開了法庭，而法官也允許強曼森自由離開了。

p. 40–41 隔天，馬德琳鎮長去探視芳婷。當她看到他時，她要求去看柯賽特。

「現在還不行。妳這麼虛弱怎麼見她？妳要先好起來才行。」他說。

接著，賈維警探走進屋內，芳婷以為警察是要來逮捕她的，她很害怕。但是馬德琳鎮長說：「他不是來抓妳的。」然後，他對賈維警探說：「給我三天的時間，去帶回她的小孩就好，接著你就可以把我送進牢裡。」

「我不會給你三天的時間逃跑的。」賈維警探說。

「但是我的孩子！」芳婷哭喊著。

「閉嘴！妳這個骯髒的妓女！」賈維警探大吼：「這個人不是馬德琳市長，他也不會把妳的女兒帶回來給妳。他是一個名叫尚萬強的危險罪犯，他很快就要入獄了！」

芳婷倒回她的枕頭上，僵直地躺著。尚萬強跑到她的床邊。她死了。「你的話害死了她！」他對賈維警探大吼。

「現在跟我回到警局，否則我就叫我的手下用武力逮捕你。」賈維說。

尚萬強親吻芳婷的額頭，然後對警察說：「我現在準備好了，走吧。」

p. 42–43 被逮捕兩天後，尚萬強從牢裡逃走了。他設法把窗戶上的欄杆弄壞，然後消失在夜色裡。

1823 年的聖誕節，康乃迪家客棧的生意非常好。客人們大聲地吃吃喝喝，而已經八歲的柯賽特就坐在她平常待的廚房桌子底下。她一身破爛，正在為康乃迪家的兩個女兒織著羊毛長襪。

一天夜裡，康乃迪太太命令柯賽特頂著寒冷的天氣外出提水。當她要出門時，康乃迪太太給了她一個銅板，要她順便去買些麵包。

柯賽特走過黑暗的樹林，來到溪邊。當她用大木桶汲水時，沒有注意到康乃迪太太給她的銅板正從她口袋裡的一個洞滾出來，掉進冰冷的水裡。

然後，她開始使勁地拉著裝滿水的沉重水桶，準備穿過樹林，走上小山丘，回到客棧。那個水桶非常重，所以她每走幾步路，就得停下來休息一下。

p. 44–45 突然間，一隻大手從空中伸下來拎起那個水桶。柯賽特抬頭看到一個高大的老人站在那裡。

「對一個像妳這麼小的孩子來說，這個水桶太重了。」這個人邊說，邊用和藹的眼神看著她。

柯賽特一點也不怕這個人，她相信他的眼神。他們一起穿過村莊往回走。他們一邊走著，柯賽特一邊說著她和康乃迪一家生活的點點滴滴。當他們走近客棧時，他把水桶交給她，然後兩人一起走進了那家客棧。

「妳為什麼去那麼久？」康乃迪太太生氣地說。

「我……我碰到這位需要地方過夜的人。」柯賽特想著一定會挨打而害怕地回答。康乃迪太太安排那個老人坐下，並給了他一杯酒，然後問柯賽特：「我叫妳買的麵包呢？」

「我……我忘記買了，太太。」

「那我給妳的錢呢？」

柯賽特找遍了她的口袋，但銅板不見了。她的臉變得慘白。突然那個老人拿起一個硬幣。

「夫人，這是我剛剛在地板上看到的，一定是從那孩子的口袋裡掉出來的。」康乃迪太太拿著硬幣走開了。

p. 46-47 隔天一早，那個老人對康乃迪夫婦說：「你們好像沒有寬裕的錢來好好照顧這個孩子，可不可以讓我帶走她？」

「我們非常愛她，」康乃迪先生說：「我們不能讓你以低於一千五百法郎的代價把她帶走。」

那個老人爽快地給了他三張五百法郎的紙鈔，並說：「現在把柯賽特交給我。」

老人給了她一些漂亮的新衣服，然後他們手牽著手前往巴黎。柯賽特並不知道這個人是誰，但她欣慰地感覺到，這個人是上帝派來守護她的。他就是尚萬強。

尚萬強帶著柯賽特來到巴黎郊外一棟很大的舊大樓。柯賽特在他的臂彎中睡著了。他帶著她上去他從賈維警探那裡逃走後就租下的屋子裡。

對柯賽特和尚萬強來說，日子開始充滿了幸福。對他來說，這是二十五年來第一次，他不再獨自一人生活在世界上，他找到了愛。

p. 48–49 一天晚上，尚萬強聽到有人在他房外的樓梯間，他跑到鑰匙孔一看，看到了一個熟悉的外套背影走下樓梯。「是賈維。」他心中暗想。

隔天，他開始準備離開屋子，去一個更安全的地方。那天夜裡，當他們在滿月的月光下，沿著狹窄的街道走著時，尚萬強發現有四個人遠遠地跟蹤他們。

他轉頭一看，藉著月光，清楚地看到賈維警探的臉。他緊握柯賽特的手，開始迂迴地穿行在複雜的小巷中。

在走進一條長巷後，他來到了一個死胡同。一邊是門窗緊閉的高樓，而另一邊則是高聳的圍牆。他自己可以爬過牆，但他要怎麼帶著柯賽特攀過去呢？

然後，他看到一座街燈，便想到一個方法。他打開街燈底座的箱子，拉出幾條電線，把線綁在柯賽特的腰上，爬上那道牆，然後再把柯賽特拉上來。牆的另一邊是一棵樹，就在那四個人追上時，他把柯賽特壓低到樹枝裡，自己也翻過那座牆。

p. 52–53 ## 人物的原型

這部小說裡的某些人物是來自真實的人物事件。

維克多・雨果曾聽過一個善良神父密歐里斯的事蹟。他曾收留一個剛被釋放的囚犯過夜，而那個囚犯回報神父的，卻是將他的銀器偷走。但密歐里斯卻告訴警察們，是他將那些值錢的東西送給他的。這個真實故事就是出現在《悲慘世界》中的 1806 年笛涅大主教事件。這個真實人物的慷慨與仁慈，也成為了法國的傳奇故事。

至於尚萬強這個角色，也是來自一個真實人物。作者雨果對於社會公義與法國的刑事體系非常感興趣，他曾造訪一些犯人，與他們進行對談。賈思就是其中一位，他告訴雨果，為了餵養自己的孩子，他闖進一棟屋子裡偷麵包，因此被送進監獄。

　　但是不同於小說裡的尚萬強的是，賈思因為在獄中殺死一個獄卒而被判死刑。雨果非常同情賈思，因為那個獄卒對賈思非常殘暴。雨果認為賈思一開始就不該被關。在他的作品《悲慘世界》中，雨果想藉著呈現導致刑罰的一連串事件，來對最後判決結果的公正性提出質疑。

　　其他來自真實人物的角色，還包括柯賽特和馬里歐。雨果，那個初嚐戀愛滋味的年輕完美主義的自己，其實就是馬里歐這個角色的來源依據；而他的妻子，顯然就是柯賽特這個角色的翻版。

第三章　巴黎人

p.54~55　1815 年六月，在滑鐵盧之役後的一個晚上，一個強盜悄悄地從戰場上死掉的士兵身上，偷走了所有的錢和珠寶。在月光下，他看到了一隻戴著金戒指的手指。當他拿走那只戒指時，那隻手抓住了他的外套。他把那個軀體從成堆的死屍中拉出來，發現那是一名還活著的法國軍官。

　　「謝謝你救了我的命，你叫什麼名字？」那名軍官問。

　　「康乃迪。」那個強盜回答說。

　　那名軍官說：「我永遠不會忘記你的名字，也請你記住我的名字，我叫蓬梅西。」

　　後來，強盜帶走那個人的手錶和皮夾，就不見了。而名叫喬治‧蓬梅西的軍官有個兒子叫馬里歐。母親已經過世的馬里歐和他的外公住在一起。他的外公是名叫葛萊姆的有錢人，但是葛萊姆非常討厭他的女婿，也就是馬里歐的父親。

　　在喬治‧蓬梅西從傷勢中復元後，葛萊姆給了他一些錢，叫他遠離他自己的兒子。蓬梅西接受了這個提議，因為他希望自己的兒子能過好日子。

p. 56–57 多年以來，葛萊姆一直跟馬里歐說他的父親是個壞蛋。但是當馬里歐十七歲時，他知道了真相，他的父親是位勇敢的軍人。馬里歐四處尋找他的父親，但是當他找到時，他已經去世了。馬里歐只從他父親那裡拿到一封信：

> 給我親愛的兒子：
>
> 　　在滑鐵盧時，我的命是一位名叫康乃迪的人所救的。我相信他應該在巴黎附近的蒙佛梅村裡經營一家小客棧。如果你找到這個人，我要你盡可能地幫助他。

　　當葛萊姆發現馬里歐去探訪他父親的墓園時，他們起了很大的爭執，然後葛萊姆就把馬里歐趕出了家門。

　　之後三年裡，馬里歐住在巴黎郊區一棟舊建築的一個小房間裡。碰巧的是，那就是尚萬強和柯賽特八年前住過的同一間屋子。

　　馬里歐幾乎沒賺到什麼錢，但還夠維生。他的外公常想要寄錢給他，但是他都拒絕了。馬里歐非常痛恨外公對待自己父親的殘酷方式。

p. 58–59 馬里歐是個俊俏的年輕人，但是他生性十分害羞。他過著讀書、寫作，和每天散步的寧靜生活。

　　有時在他散步途中，他注意到有個老人和一個年輕女孩，總是坐在盧森堡公園的同一張長椅上。這女孩大約十三、四歲，都穿著同一件黑色的洋裝。但馬里歐注意到的是她那一雙可愛的藍眼睛。

　　因為某個原因，馬里歐不再去盧森堡公園。當他一年後又回到那裡時，他們仍然坐在相同的位置上。唯一不同的是，那個一年前瘦小的女孩，已經變成一位美麗的妙齡女子。她有著柔軟的褐髮、平滑白皙的肌膚、深邃的藍眼睛，和燦爛的笑容。

有一天當他經過時，他們的眼神交會了。他覺得他的人生起了變化。他開始每天注意那個老人與女孩。他太常跟著他們，因此那個老人開始對他起疑，而且也開始減少到公園的次數，有時候身邊還不帶著那個女孩。

當那個老人和女孩不再到公園時，馬里歐開始變得消沉，因此他想要找出他們住的地方。最後，他終於得知他們住在魁斯特路街尾的一棟小房子裡。

p. 60~61 馬里歐開始跟蹤他們回家，並隔著透出亮光的窗戶看著他們。當他得以瞥見那個女孩一眼時，他的心跳開始加速。在他造訪那棟小屋的第八個夜裡，窗裡的燈光不再亮著。當他看到這個情形時，他敲了隔壁鄰居的門，詢問他們去哪裡了。

「他們搬走了。」那鄰居說。然後就當著馬里歐的面，把門砰地一聲關上。

夏天過了，秋天也走了，馬里歐再也沒有見到老人或那位他愛上的年輕女孩。他沮喪地在街頭漫步，像一隻迷路的小狗。缺少了那位年輕女孩，生命對他來說似乎毫無意義。

後來有一天，馬里歐在他家附近發現有個裝著四封信的小包裹。當他讀著信時，他察覺到那可能是由四個不同的人所寫的，但它們卻全出自同一個筆跡。那四封信發出廉價菸草的臭味，而且內容全都是來要錢的。

隔天早上，馬里歐的門上傳來了敲門聲。當他開門後，看到一個瘦弱的女孩，一臉病容，還缺了牙齒。她是隔壁鄰居的女兒。她遞給他一封她父親寫給他的信：

親愛的鄰居：

　　我衷心地記得你六個月前已經付過房租了。但是現在我的妻子生病，我們也四天沒吃過東西了。我拜託您再度發揮您的愛心和慷慨。

　　　　　　　　　　　　　您誠摯的瓊耶敬上

`p. 62-63` 馬里歐發現這個筆跡和廉價的菸草味，和他前一晚發現的信件一樣，都是來自隔壁那個窮困的家庭。

　　從他們成為鄰居的幾個月來，他從沒注意過瓊耶一家人。但是現在他知道了，瓊耶先生的工作就是寫一些不實的信件，向那些他以為比較有錢的人要錢。

　　當馬里歐讀信時，那個女孩一直看著他。現在她向他靠近，並把她冷冰冰的手放在他肩上。

　　「馬里歐先生，你知道嗎？你是位俊俏的男孩。雖然你從沒注意過我，但我發現你看起來總是很落寞的樣子。」

　　「我想我這裡有一些你們的東西。」馬里歐邊說，邊移開身體，避開她的碰觸。他把裝著四封信的那個包裹交給她。

　　「喔，是的。我到處在找這些東西。」她拿出其中一封信說：「這封是要給那位每天上教堂的老人的。如果我動作快一點，就可以在街上堵到他，他可能會給我足夠吃晚飯的錢吧！」

`p. 64-65` 馬里歐從他的口袋拿出了一個銅板，給了那個女孩。

　　她大叫：「啊哈！這足夠吃兩天了！你真是個天使，馬里歐先生。」然後，她笑著從馬里歐桌上抓了一塊乾麵包，便離開了。

馬里歐發現，雖然他靠著微薄的金錢過活，但是一直到認識了隔壁這一個不幸的家庭，他才知道什麼叫做貧窮。當他還在想那個糟糕的家庭時，他注意到隔著他家和隔壁家中間的牆上，有個三角形的小洞。他決定要觀察他們的一舉一動。

馬里歐站在櫥櫃上，把他的眼睛湊近洞口。瓊耶家又髒又臭，和馬里歐毫無陳設、乾淨的住處完全不同。那裡唯一的家具，就是一張壞掉的桌子、一張椅子，和兩張髒亂的床鋪，桌上還有一些破盤子。

桌子那裡坐著一個老人、抽著菸斗，正在寫信。一個看得出原本是紅色頭髮、但現在已經變成白髮的高大女人，就坐在壁爐旁。而一個瘦弱又滿臉病容的女孩，就坐在一張床上。馬里歐對他所看到的景象感到非常地難過。

p. 66–67 馬里歐打算不再看下去了，但是那個來過他房裡的女孩突然間跳著跑進瓊耶家的家門。

「他來了！」她開心地大叫。

「誰來了？」她父親問。

「那個每天都跟他女兒上教堂的老人啊！我在街上看到他們，而且他們就要來了。我是跑在他們之前來告訴大家的，他們兩分鐘後就到了。」

「好女兒。」瓊耶先生接著說：「快！快把火弄熄！」

瓊耶先生用腳把椅子弄壞的同時，那女孩就把水倒在壁爐的火上。他叫另一個小女兒去把窗戶打破，那女孩用她的拳頭擊破玻璃，這讓她的手臂傷得很嚴重。她滿身是血地跑向床上。

「太好了，我們看起來愈慘，那位善良的紳士就會給我們愈多錢。」

一會兒，門上傳來敲門聲。瓊耶先生開門後，頭幾乎要碰到地上地向他們鞠躬。那個老人和女孩走進了屋子裡。

馬里歐一陣震撼，他就是公園裡的那個老人！而她就是他愛上的那個女孩！

p. 68–69 那個老人交給瓊耶先生一個包裹，說道：「這裡是一些暖和的衣服和毯子，給你的家人。」

「先生，謝謝您。就像您所看到的，我們沒有食物，也沒有暖氣。我太太病得很重，而我的女兒又在她工作的工廠裡傷了手臂。」

那個手臂受傷的女孩痛苦地哀叫著。善良的老人從他的口袋拿了一個銅板放在桌上。

「我現在身上就只有五法郎。今天傍晚晚一點，我會再帶一些錢回來給你。」

在他們離開之後，馬里歐打算離開他的屋子去跟蹤他們。他必須知道那位漂亮的年輕女孩住在哪裡。但瓊耶家的女兒又走回到他門前，她走進了他的屋子。

「妳到底想要什麼？」他問。他正在生她的氣。

「今天早上你對我們很好，現在我也要對你好。」她用一種挑逗的態度說：「我願意為你做一件事。」

馬里歐想了一下。

「妳知道那個剛剛來過妳家的老人和那女孩的住址嗎？」

她看起來很失望，但還是說：「不，我不知道。但是如果您要的話，我會查出來的。」

p. 70-71 瓊耶家的女兒離開後，馬里歐發現自己已經被那個神秘年輕女孩的情感給壓倒了。接著，他又聽到瓊耶先生的聲音從牆上的洞傳過來。他跳回櫥櫃上聽著。

「你確定是他們嗎？」瓊耶太太問。

「我確定。我認出他們兩個了。雖然！已經八年過去，但我還是很確定。」

「是她？」瓊耶太太說，她的聲音充滿了憎恨：「你一定是弄錯了。那個孩子很醜的，但是這個女孩很漂亮。」

「我告訴妳，她們是同一個人。」瓊耶先生說：「他們又要再給我們一大筆錢了！當那個老人六點回來時，我要找一群朋友來這裡，一定要他們把所有的錢都交給我們，否則他就別想從這裡離開。」瓊耶先生露出邪惡的笑容。

馬里歐知道他必須救那個老人和他喜歡的女孩。他前往最近的警察局，要求和局長說話。

一位警察說：「他不在，我是代理負責人，我叫賈維。你有什麼需要？」

p. 72-73 馬里歐告訴那個警探有關瓊耶的邪惡計畫。當賈維聽到那個地點時，他的眼睛亮了起來。他交給馬里歐一把小手槍。

「當你聽到騷動開始時，就從你的窗戶開槍。我會在附近，一等到這個訊號，我就會帶著我的手下衝進去。」

回到他的屋子後，馬里歐緊張地等待著。在牆壁的另一頭，瓊耶先生在火堆裡放了一根金屬棒，並準備了一把長尖刀。他還在他的窗外放了一條繩梯，萬一需要趕快逃跑時就可以使用。

六點整時，大門開了，那個老人走了進來。他把四個硬幣放在桌上：「這是讓你繳房租和買食物的。你還需要什麼嗎？」

在聊了幾分鐘後，瓊耶先生叫來了他的朋友，三個人帶著金屬棍棒衝進屋內。那個老人拿起壞掉的椅子準備應戰。馬里歐也準備要開槍。

　　「你認不出我嗎？」瓊耶先生問那個老人。

　　「對。」那個老人回答。

　　「我真正的名字不是瓊耶，是康乃迪。現在你認識我了吧？」

　　那個老人顫抖著。

`p. 74–75` 一聽到「康乃迪」這個名字，馬里歐幾乎從他站的櫥櫃上跌下來。那是他父親救命恩人的名字。突然間，他沒辦法照他原先計畫開槍通知那個警探了。

　　「八年前，你帶著柯賽特離開我們。她曾為我們帶來很多錢，而你就是我們所有問題的源頭。」

　　「你只是個骯髒的罪犯。」那個老人說。

　　「你認為我是個罪犯？我可是在滑鐵盧之役中救了一位軍官的命呢。讓我來給你一個教訓。」

　　那個老人想跳出窗外，但是那三個人把他抓了下來。馬里歐不知道該怎麼辦。康乃迪拔出了他的長刀，準備要殺死那個老人。

　　但是突然間，門猛然地被打開，警探賈維帶著十五名警察出現了。他們開始逮捕屋裡的所有人。在一團混亂當中，那個老人成功地從窗戶逃走了。在他們注意到他不見前，他早就已經跑掉了。

[第四章] 戀人與革命

p. 78–79 出於對他父親遺願的尊重，馬里歐不想提出不利於康乃迪的證據。他搬出了他的住處，和他的朋友恩佐拉一起住。

有一天，馬里歐坐在河邊，夢想著他的摯愛時，聽到了一個熟悉的聲音。他抬頭一看，認出了那是康乃迪家的女兒，艾潘妮。

「我終於找到你了，」她說：「我到處在找你。」

馬里歐一句話都沒說。

「你看到我好像不太開心。」她接著說：「但是如果我想要的話，我可以讓你開心起來。」

「妳要怎麼做？」

「我拿到了你要的地址了。」

他的心跳了一下，整個人跳起來，然後抓住她的手。

「我們立刻就走吧！」他叫著：「答應我，妳絕對不會把那個地址告訴妳父親。」

那天晚上，柯賽特獨自一人待在尚萬強一年前買的房子裡。那是一棟小房子，位在一條偏僻的小路上，有著既小又荒涼的花園。尚萬強剛好出門辦事不在家。柯賽特正在彈鋼琴，她聽到花園裡傳來腳步聲，但當她探頭看時，花園裡卻空無一人。

p. 80–81 隔天早上，柯賽特在附近的長椅上發現了一顆石頭。當她把石頭拿起來時，看到有個信封裡裝著一本寫滿情詩的小筆記本。她反覆讀著那些詩，欣賞詩中所訴說的一切。她記得那位總是在盧森堡公園看著她的年輕帥哥，她知道，這些詩是他寫的。

那天晚上，柯賽特穿上她最好的洋裝，並將自己的頭髮梳理得很美。接著，她走進花園裡等著。忽然間，她覺得自己被注視了。那就是他！他瘦了，他的皮膚也比她記憶中更蒼白，但那真的是他。

「原諒我注意妳那麼久。自從那天妳在公園裡看了我一眼之後，沒有妳，我就失了魂。」年輕人說。

柯賽特被他的話震懾住了，感到一陣昏眩並往後倒去。他抓住她，將她緊緊抱在臂彎中。

「妳也愛我嗎？」他問。

「我當然愛你。」她說：「你知道我是愛你的。」

他們坐在滿天星星所織成的銀毯下親吻著。

p. 82-83 1832 年的整個五月裡，柯賽特和馬里歐每天都在那個隱密小屋的花園裡約會。他們整天都握著對方的手，凝視著彼此的眼睛。馬里歐甚至開始想著，自己可能會因為太過幸福而發狂。

在一個滿天星星的美好夜裡，馬里歐看到柯賽特鬱鬱不樂地坐在花園裡。

「怎麼了？」馬里歐問。

「我父親說我們必須再次搬家。他吩咐我要打包所有的東西，一個星期內前往倫敦。」

「妳會和他一起去嗎？」馬里歐冷冷地問。

「我還能怎麼辦呢？」

「妳要離開我了。」

「噢！馬里歐，不要這麼殘酷！」她說：「你也可以一起來啊！」

他喊著：「但是我沒錢，要有錢才能去英國啊！不過我想到一個方法了。我明天不會來這裡。」

「為什麼不會？」柯賽特哭了：「你要做什麼？」

「別擔心，我後天就會回來。我保證我會在晚上九點以前在這裡和妳碰面。」

p. 84-85 馬里歐的外公葛萊姆已經九十歲了。他非常悲傷，因為他已經好幾年沒看到他的孫子了。他因為太驕傲，無法承認自己做錯了，但他暗自希望他心愛的孫子有一天能回來。

那是一個六月的傍晚，當葛萊姆先生凝視著壁爐裡的火，悲傷地思念著馬里歐時，一個僕人突然走進來問道：「先生，您願意接見馬里歐先生的探訪嗎？」

老人顫抖了一下，然後用平靜的口吻說：「帶他進來。」

當年輕人進來後，他問：「你為什麼來這裡？你是來向我道歉的嗎？」

馬里歐隱藏了他的無奈，回答：「不是的。我是來請您為我的婚禮祝福的。」

「你才二十一歲就想結婚了。你現在賺多少錢？」

「我現在沒有錢。」

「那那個女孩應該很有錢囉。」

「我不知道。」

「一個沒有錢、沒有工作的二十一歲年輕人，當你的妻子上市場時，一定非精打細算不可吧！」

「外公，拜託您！我非常愛她，我請您祝福我們！」

老人露出了憎惡的笑容：「不可能！」

p. 86-87 馬里歐既苦惱又疲累。當他回到恩佐拉的住所時，恩佐拉正和一些革命黨的朋友在一起。那一群人非常激動，因為街頭將展開一場政府軍與革命人士的交戰。

在他們離開後，馬里歐拿出了賈維警探在二月時給他的手槍，把它放進口袋，在街頭漫步著。九點時，他爬進了柯賽特的花園，但是她並未依約出現。屋子沒有任何燈光，窗戶也緊閉著。馬里歐煩躁地用拳頭搥著牆壁。

等到他完全沒有力氣時，他坐了下來。「她走了。」他喃喃自語。除了一死，他已經沒有什麼事可做了。

沒多久，他聽到一個叫他名字的聲音從街頭傳來，「馬里歐先生！」

「誰？」馬里歐回應。

「馬里歐先生，你的朋友在香瑞里路的路障那裡等你。他們很快就要和軍隊開戰了。」

當馬里歐越過牆時，他看到康乃迪家女兒艾潘妮的身影跑進了陰暗處。

p. 88–89 1832 年春天，巴黎陷入一種大變革的狀態。當專橫的查理十世在 1830 年被和平的革命運動推翻後，路易菲利普國王取得了王位。新的領導者不了解窮人的需求和力量，也不懂言論自由的概念。他還不時地派遣士兵，去攻擊那些公開進行抗議的平民們。

工人和窮人的情緒被激怒了。當拉馬克將軍過世時，他們的不滿爆發了。拉馬克將軍深受法國人的愛戴，因為他不但是民主制度的忠實擁護者，也是拿破崙一世的支持者。

喪禮平靜地開始，但是當一大群抗議者想從軍隊手中奪走棺木時，雙方就開戰了，有人因此身亡。巴黎陷入對抗衝突的狀態。

恩佐拉和朋友們在市集的一家酒舖外設置路障。在他們進行的途中，一個高大白髮的陌生人加入了他們的行列，其他的男孩們也獻上了他們的力量，其中一個就是艾潘妮。她做了一身男孩的打扮，這樣她才能留下來，在抗爭中幫忙。

p. 90–91 設好路障後，恩佐拉和他的朋友停下來休息。他們總共只有五十個人，卻準備要和六萬名士兵對抗。他們自己也知道成功的機會很小。

當他們坐著喝酒時，恩佐拉開始懷疑那個高大的白髮陌生人是間諜。「你是被派來暗中刺探我們的警察吧？快承認！」恩佐拉說。

那個人想否認，但最後還是說出了實話，他的確是警方的間諜。

「我叫賈維。」那個人說。

恩佐拉將他俘虜，並把他綁在柱子上，然後告訴他：「在路障倒塌前兩分鐘，我們會射殺你。」

當馬里歐走近路障時，軍隊就開始發動攻擊了。

子彈颼颼地掠過每一處，馬里歐看到一名士兵正要攻擊恩佐拉。他從口袋裡拔出槍，殺了士兵。但是當他在救恩佐拉的時候，他並沒有看到另一名士兵正拿著槍瞄準他。那個士兵開了槍，就在那一刻，一個男孩跳到槍口前救了馬里歐。四周都是反抗者和士兵的死屍。

p. 92–93 戰爭持續了一段時間後，政府士兵控制了路障的頂部。這時，每個人都聽到了一個聲音：「後退，否則我就點燃這一桶火藥，我們大家一起死！」那是馬里歐。他把火炬放低對著砲筒口，所有的士兵都跟著撤退。

恩佐拉萬分高興地看到馬里歐，他們倆擁抱著。就在那時，馬里歐聽到一個微弱的聲音叫著他的名字，他往下一看，看到穿著男裝、滿身是血的艾潘妮。

「別怕，」他對她說：「我們會找醫生來救妳！」

「不，太遲了。」她說，血像紅酒一樣從她身上滲出。她把自己的頭放在他的膝蓋上，要求他在她死後親吻她的額頭。馬里歐答應了。

接著，她又說：「我無法對你說謊，我的口袋裡有一封柯賽特要我拿給你的信。但我嫉妒她，所以本來想把信扣留下來的。我愛你啊。」

說完她就斷氣了。馬里歐親吻了她的額頭後，讀起了柯賽特的信：

吾愛：

　　我們現在必須離開這間屋子了，我們今晚要去荷馬路七號。一個星期後，我們就要搬去英國了。我希望能再見到你。

獻上我所有的愛
柯賽特　六月四日

p. 94–95 馬里歐親吻了那封信，雖然他還是覺得自己會在這個革命之夜喪生，但他決定寄出最後一封信給她。他拿出筆記本，寫下：

最為親愛的柯賽特：

　　我們是不可能結婚了。我的外公拒絕給予我們祝福。我曾試著去見妳，但妳已經離開了。現在這裡的情勢很危急，我可能過不了今晚這一關。但我對妳的愛至死不渝，我的靈魂將永遠伴妳左右。

永遠的愛
馬里歐

他把信折好，寫上她的住址。一個小男孩剛好經過，馬里歐要他趕緊幫忙送信。那個孩子拿了信後，就跑進黑暗中。

尚萬強很難過，他和柯賽特有史以來第一次吵架。她不想搬離原來的屋子。現在在他們的新家裡，兩個人一句話也不說就上床睡覺了。

隔天，尚萬強聽說了城裡的戰事，但他一點也不在乎，他很高興他們很快就要去英國了。但是某個東西吸引了他的目光，從鏡子裡，他看到一張吸墨紙，那是柯賽特用來吸乾信上的墨水的。他開始讀起上面的內容，這才知道她戀愛了。

p. 96–97 尚萬強很生氣，他有一種被背叛的感覺，因為有人要把他唯一的愛搶走。他知道一定是那個他們常常在盧森堡公園看到的年輕人。他走出去，站在屋前的台階上，他的心燃燒著憤怒的熾火。

當小男孩帶著要給柯賽特的信走近時，尚萬強正想著要如何報復那個年輕人。他收了信，讀了起來。「我可能過不了今晚這一關」這些字眼讓他感到痛快。只要那個人一死，就能解決他的問題了。搞不好，那個人已經死了。

但是尚萬強知道，為了柯賽特的幸福，他應該要去救那個人，雖然他比全世界任何人都還要恨他。

三十分鐘後，尚萬強穿上他國民警衛隊的舊制服，塞了一把上膛的槍在口袋裡，前往巴黎的市集。

當晚，在路障的後面有三十七名反抗者存活了下來。當他們把所有的死屍聚集起來時，找到了四套國民警衛隊的制服。這些制服可以讓那群人裡面已婚的人偽裝撤退。

p. 98–99 因為只有四套制服，但卻有五個已婚的男人，所以那些人開始爭論起來，到底誰應該留在原地繼續戰鬥。每個人都想當那個犧牲的人。然後，第五套國民警衛隊制服掉在他們面前了，那是尚萬強的。「現在五個人都可以走了。」他說。他加入了路障後的那群人，沒多久，士兵開始朝他們發射砲彈，路障在攻擊下崩塌。

戰火一開始時，尚萬強就問恩佐拉，他能不能當那個處決賈維警探的人。恩佐拉說：「你幫我們帶來這套制服，你應該得到獎賞，好吧！把他帶到小巷的後面，開槍處決他。」

尚萬強帶著賈維走到後面的巷子裡，在附近整排屍體最上面的是艾潘妮死去的屍體。「我想我認得那個女孩。」賈維悲哀地說：「現在你可以報仇了。」

尚萬強拔出槍對空中開火，然後他拿出刀子，割斷了綁在賈維腰上的繩子，「你可以離開了。」他說。

賈維說：「這太難堪了，我寧願你殺了我。」

p. 102–103 故事背景

為了更了解《悲慘世界》這個故事，認識這個故事的歷史和哲學背景是很重要的。十八世紀的法國見證了正在發展的哲學上的變動，與政治上的動盪不安。因為一些激進作家如伏爾泰、休姆等人的作品，人民也逐漸地了解社會公平正義的概念。

他們作品裡所宣傳的理念，鼓勵了讀者去挑戰社會中死板的宗教傳統和原則。此舉間接造成了法國大革命與拿破崙時代，而這兩項重要事件也是《悲慘世界》情節中的背景與歷史脈絡來源。

這部作品也記錄了當時哲學觀的變遷。人們想要遠離無法容忍罪惡的冷酷宗教教條，改採更寬容、更有愛心的方式。這個轉變稱為「啟蒙運動」。這個運動產生了上帝與原罪並不存在的想法，認為唯一的真理就是人有道德上的自由。

但是這個自由是有限制的，因為如此一來，剝奪他人的自由就會是錯誤的。因此有人可能會問，那我們該如何度過我們的一生呢？

在《悲慘世界》中，雨果告訴我們，應該先認識自己對彼此的責任，包括人與人之間，以及在社會這個團體中的各種責任。這個概念也很清楚地表現在故事中那位主教與尚萬強的行為上。

[第五章] 贖罪

p. 104–105 士兵們集結人馬衝向路障，反抗者一個接一個地倒下。馬里歐被射到肩膀，然後他感到有人抓住他。在他失去意識之際，他以為自己會被士兵抓住，並被處決。恩佐拉在一陣彈雨中死命地揮舞著他的劍。他是最後一個死掉的反抗者。

馬里歐並沒有被囚禁起來。在他被射昏後，尚萬強抓住他，把他拉到路障後面的小巷弄裡。

面對不斷逼近的軍隊，似乎已經沒有退路。尚萬強環顧四周，想到了個方法。路上有一個被鐵架蓋住的洞，尚萬強抬起鐵架，把馬里歐扛上他的肩膀，往下爬進了巴黎的下水道。

下水道裡又滑又暗，尚萬強奮力地扛著馬里歐，舉步維艱地越過流動的污水，走進前方的暗處之中。

在走了很長的一段時間之後，他不得不休息一下。他停下來幫馬里歐包紮流血的傷口。他在那個年輕人的口袋裡發現一張紙條：

> 我是馬里歐‧蓬梅西。請將我的屍體送到我外公葛萊姆位於瑪黑區菲得杜卡維爾大道六號的家中。

p. 106–107 尚萬強記下住址，繼續穿越污水往河流前進。幾個小時之後，他終於看到長長隧道盡頭的燈火。但是當他走到盡頭時，隔在下水道與自由之間的鐵門被鎖住了。尚萬強發出了絕望的叫喊，已經沒有路可以出去了。

他突然感到有一隻手在肩上，那是康乃迪先生。他從監獄逃出來，跑進了下水道。他給尚萬強看了他偷來可以開鐵門的鑰匙。

康乃迪說：「我看到你殺了這個人，如果你給我一半從他口袋偷來的錢，我就讓你越過這道鐵門。」

尚萬強什麼都沒說。他伸手進他的口袋裡，給了康乃迪三十法郎。「你為了這一點點錢就殺人。你真是個人渣！」康乃迪邊開鎖邊說，然後他就像老鼠一樣匆忙地跑進下水道。

尚萬強爬上河岸，來到了上面的世界。他停下腳步，潑了一些水在馬里歐的臉上。但是那裡站著另一個人，那是賈維。那個警察從康乃迪逃獄後，就一直跟蹤著康乃迪。

p. 108–109 「請幫我帶這個人回家，他傷得很嚴重。」尚萬強說。賈維看起來不太高興，但還是答應幫他。他們把馬里歐安放在一輛馬車上，並且告訴車伕地址。在葛萊姆家的門口，尚萬強告訴賈維，在他將那個男孩送進屋裡後，他就可以逮捕他。但是當尚萬強返回正在等著的馬車時，賈維警探已經不見了。

當葛萊姆先生看到馬里歐毫無生氣的身體時，他哭喊著：「他死了，這個笨蛋！他這麼做是為了懲罰我。」

後來一個醫生前來幫馬里歐檢查。

醫生說：「他應該還活著。他身上的傷口並不嚴重，但是他的頭部有幾道比較深的傷口。」

「噢，我的孫子！」葛萊姆欣喜地喊著：「你終究還是活下來了！」

隔天早上，賈維的屍體在河裡被人發現。他一直因為無法理解尚萬強的善意與寬宏大量而鬱鬱不樂。他自殺了。

p. 110–111 馬里歐接下來花了三個月的時間才康復。

　　有一天他說：「外公，我還是打算娶柯賽特。」

　　「當然，孩子。」葛萊姆說。自從他的孫子死裡逃生後，他就變得和藹多了。「一切都安排好了，她正等著你按照醫生的吩咐康復起來。我得認識一下她和她的父親，我想她一定是位迷人的女孩。」

　　馬里歐喜出望外。當天稍晚，柯賽特和她的父親來訪。她的父親還帶著異常緊張的微笑。

　　他們的婚禮安排在隔年的二月舉行。這對快樂的夫婦決定在結婚後和葛萊姆先生住在一起。

　　對馬里歐來說，除了準備結婚，還有兩件重要的事要做。他想找到康乃迪。雖然他知道那個傢伙是個可惡的盜賊，但他還是無論如何都想要尊重父親的遺願；另外，他想要找到被射傷那晚救了他的人。他常對柯賽特和尚萬強提到這件事，但尚萬強總是保持沉默。

p. 112–113 婚禮那晚十分美好，唯一讓柯賽特覺得不開心的事，就是尚萬強說他覺得不舒服，在宴席開始之前就先回家了。

　　尚萬強在家裡痛哭。他還記得十年前，那個他從康乃迪家救出來的小女孩。他感到悲傷不已，因為他已經不再是她生命中最重要的人了。然後，他想起自己是尚萬強，一個在牢裡度過十九年的犯人，一個從仁慈的主教家偷了銀器的人。

　　這些事柯賽特都不知道，如果她和馬里歐知道的話，他就會失去他們對他的愛與尊敬。但如果他不把真相說出來的話，他覺得自己會失去靈魂。

隔天，尚萬強去找馬里歐談話。他告訴這個年輕人有關他過去的一切。

　　「你必須答應我不告訴她。」尚萬強說。

　　「我不會告訴她的。」馬里歐說，「但是你不應該再時時待在她身邊了。」

　　「那你必須讓我偶爾見見她，」尚萬強哀求說：「沒有她，我就沒有活著的理由了。」

　　「你可以在每天傍晚和她短暫地見一下面。」馬里歐回答。

p. 114–115 　　每天傍晚，尚萬強就在一間只有兩張椅子和爐火的小房間裡和柯賽特相會。她拜託他和他們住在一起，但是他總是婉拒。他甚至不再讓她叫他「父親」。「妳現在有丈夫，不再需要父親了。」

　　但就像她現在稱呼他「尚萬強先生」一樣，對她來說，他漸漸變成了另外一個人。她開始愈來愈少接受他的來訪。在一段時間後，他們甚至不再碰面了。

　　馬里歐覺得，讓尚萬強離開柯賽特的生活是一件好事。在他私下對尚萬強的調查中，他發現尚萬強的財富都是來自一位已經失蹤的富人瑪德琳鎮長。在知道這件事後，他不再讓柯賽特用任何尚萬強給她的錢。

　　接著，有一天傍晚，有個僕人送一封信來給馬里歐，並說那個寫信的人就在大廳等著。那封信有著廉價菸草的味道，還有一些熟悉的筆跡。當他看到那位訪客時，他很驚訝地發現是康乃迪。那個差勁的人是來要錢的。

p. 116-117 「我有一些關於您岳父的有趣消息要告訴你。」康乃迪先生說。

「我已經知道他的事了。」馬里歐說。

「那個您以為是您妻子的監護人，其實是個叫做尚萬強的殺人犯和小偷。」

馬里歐說：「我知道，我知道他搶了一個叫馬德琳鎮長的有錢工廠老闆，還殺了賈維警探。」

康乃迪說：「不對，他並沒有搶馬德琳鎮長的錢，他就是馬德琳鎮長。而且他也沒有殺賈維警探，賈維是自殺的。」

他給馬里歐看一份有關那位警探自殺的剪報。「但是他的確殺了一個年輕人，我看到他扛著他的屍體穿過下水道，我甚至還有那個年輕人的衣角可以當證據。」

接著，康乃迪就給馬里歐看了染血的外套碎片。馬里歐認出那是他的衣服。

「那個年輕人就是我！」馬里歐大叫說。

突然間他懂了，原來尚萬強就是那個救他一命的人。

p. 118-119 馬里歐給了康乃迪一筆錢，足夠讓他帶著他餘留下的女兒亞薩瑪去美國，開始他們的新生活。

「妳父親就是那個救了我的人！我們得馬上去見他！」

當他們敲著尚萬強的門時，他們聽到一個微弱的聲音說：「進來。」

「父親！」柯賽特哭著跑向那個沉沉地陷在椅子裡的老人。

「所以你決定原諒我了。」尚萬強說。

馬里歐流著內疚和羞愧的眼淚說：「我好慚愧啊！尚萬強，您為什麼不告訴我，我欠您一命呢？」

「我不想你去感激一個毫無價值的罪犯啊！」尚萬強說。

「您一定要來和我們住在一起。」馬里歐說。

「這次您不能拒絕了。」柯賽特說。但是當她握住他的手時，她發現他雙手冰冷，「您病了嗎？父親。」

p. 120–121 「不，不是生病，」尚萬強說：「我是快死了。但是死並不足惜，枉過生命才悲哀。」

尚萬強的呼吸愈來愈困難，他指著旁邊的一張桌子。

「柯賽特，我要妳留著那幾座銀燭台。把它們送給我的人現在正在看著我們，我希望他開心。現在，柯賽特，我得說出妳母親的事情了。她的名字叫芳婷，妳絕對不可以忘記。她非常地愛妳，而且受了很多的苦。她所承受的悲傷，就像妳現在擁有的幸福一樣多。上帝就是這樣子來維持平衡的。我現在就要離開妳了，但是記得永遠要珍愛彼此。愛是生命中唯一重要的事。」

當尚萬強從雙唇間吐出最後一口氣時，柯賽特和馬里歐跪在他的身邊哭泣著。在兩座燭台的照耀下，他們看到了他臉上一抹祥和的微笑。

Answers

P. 30　**Ⓐ** ❶ (c)　❷ (d)　❸ (a)　❹ (e)　❺ (b)

　　　Ⓑ ❹ → ❷ → ❸ → ❶ → ❺

P. 31　**Ⓒ** ❶ (b)　❷ (c)

　　　Ⓓ ❶ (a)　❷ (b)　❸ (a)

P. 50　**Ⓐ** ❶ F　❷ T　❸ F　❹ F　❺ T

　　　Ⓑ ❶ (b)　❷ (e)　❸ (d)　❹ (c)　❺ (a)

P. 51　**Ⓒ** ❶ (c)　❷ (a)

　　　Ⓓ ❶ ignored　　❷ escaped　　❸ trusted
　　　　　 ❹ discovered

P. 76　**Ⓐ** ❷ → ❹ → ❶ → ❸ → ❺

　　　Ⓑ ❶ (a)　❷ (b)

P. 77　**Ⓒ** ❶ (b)　❷ (c)

　　　Ⓓ ❶ (d)　❷ (a)　❸ (b)　❹ (c)

P. 100　**Ⓐ** ❶ (d)　❷ (c)　❸ (a)　❹ (b)

　　　Ⓑ ❶ evidence　　❷ swooned　　❸ overthrown
　　　　　 ❹ supporter　　❺ retreated

P. 101　**Ⓒ** ❶ (a)　❷ (c)

　　　Ⓓ ❶ F　❷ T　❸ F　❹ T　❺ F

P. 122　**Ⓐ** ❶ (d)　❷ (c)　❸ (a)　❹ (b)

　　　Ⓑ ❶ F　❷ T　❸ F　❹ T　❺ F

P. 123　**Ⓒ** ❶ (c)　❷ (b)

　　　Ⓓ ❶ bandage　　❷ recuperating　　❸ declined
　　　　　 ❹ executed

P. 136 **(A)** **❶** This person tried to put Jean Valjean back in prison for a long time. – Javert

❷ This woman became a prostitute to earn money for her daughter. – Fantine

❸ This person hated his grandfather for treating his father so cruelly. – Marius

❹ This person's business was writing dishonest letters to wealthy people. – M. Thenardier

❺ This person's soul was given to God by the Bishop of Digne. – Jean Valjean

(B) **❶** What did the Bishop of Digne tell the police when they caught Jean Valjean? (b)

❷ Why were the revolutionaries fighting the soldiers in the summer of 1832? (c)

P. 137 **(C)** **❶** trembled, calm   **❷** argued, released

❸ Coincidentally, earlier   **❹** envelope, poems

❺ knelt, weeping

(D) **❶** After stealing the coin from the ten-year-old boy, Jean Valjean wept for the first time in nineteen years. (T)

❷ Mayor Madeline was robbed and killed by Jean Valjean. (F)

❸ The Jondrettes' younger daughter cut her arm at the factory where she worked. (F)

❹ Enjolras suspected Javert of being sent to the barricade by the police to spy on them. (T)

❺ Marius hated Jean Valjean for killing a young man in the Paris sewer. (F)

悲慘世界【二版】
Les Misérables

作者 _ 維克多・雨果（Victor Hugo）

改寫 _ Michael Robert Bradie

插圖 _ An Ji-yeon

翻譯 _ 林育珊

編輯 _ 賴祖兒 / 鄭玉瑋

作者 / 故事簡介翻譯 _ 王采翎

校對 _ 張盛傑

封面設計 _ 林書玉

排版 _ 葳豐 / 林書玉

播音員 _ Christopher Hughes,
　　　　Michael Yancey, Anna Paik

製程管理 _ 洪巧玲

發行人 _ 周均亮

出版者 _ 寂天文化事業股份有限公司

電話 _ +886-2-2365-9739

傳真 _ +886-2-2365-9835

網址 _ www.icosmos.com.tw

讀者服務 _ onlineservice@icosmos.com.tw

出版日期 _ 2020年8月 二版一刷（250201）

郵撥帳號 _ 1998620-0 寂天文化事業股份有限公司

Adaptor of "*Les Misérables*"

Michael Robert Bradie

Auburn University (BA - Communications)
a freelance writer

國家圖書館出版品預行編目資料

悲慘世界 / Victor Hugo 原著；Michael Robert
Bradie 改寫. -- 二版. -- [臺北市]：寂天文化，
2020.08　面；　公分
譯自：Les miserables
ISBN 978-986-318-933-6 (平裝附光碟片)

1. 英語 2. 讀本

805.18　　　　　　　　　　　109011341